A CHRISTMAS MELODY

Anita Stansfield

Covenant Communications, Inc.

Covenant®

OTHER BOOKS AND BOOKS ON CASSETTE
BY ANITA STANSFIELD:

First Love and Forever
First Love, Second Chances
Now and Forever
By Love and Grace
A Promise of Forever
Home for Christmas
Return to Love
To Love Again
When Forever Comes

Cover photo by Grant Heaton Productions

Published by Covenant Communications, Inc.
American Fork, Utah

Printed in the United States of America
First Printing: October 1998

05 04 03 02 01 00 99 98   10 9 8 7 6 5 4 3 2 1

Library of Congress Cataloging-in-Publication Data

Stansfield, Anita, 1961-
    A Christmas Melody : a novel / Anita Stansfield.
        p.   cm.
    ISBN 1-57734-335-2
    I. Title
    PS3569.T33354C48 1998
    813' .54--dc21   98-41060
                                          CIP

This book is dedicated to anyone who has
ever hated Christmas.

And written with heartfelt gratitude to my father. . .
for giving his children the spirit of Christmas.

I'm glad you finally got your little wagon.

Chapter One

Provo, Utah

Thanksgiving was less than two weeks away. While most people were bustling to get an early start on their Christmas shopping and making plans for family celebrations, Melody Morgan had knots in her stomach. To her, the holiday season was nothing more than a stark reminder that some people simply get cheated out of the good things in life, and some families are not worth celebrating *anything* with.

Melody frantically searched for every bit of spare change she might have, and barely came up with enough for the bus fare to get to her mother's house, a few miles from her new apartment. How she would get anywhere beyond that remained to be seen. With any luck, this visit home would turn out a little better than usual. Getting off the bus, she covered her straight, dark hair with a long scarf to protect her ears from the cold. It had yet to snow, but the cold had been bitter and relentless—one more reason to hate this time of year.

Melody walked the few blocks from the bus stop to her mother's house. Just going into the neighborhood where she had grown up made the knots in her stomach tighten. She was twenty years old, but she still couldn't think about her childhood without getting upset. She reminded herself that she was making a new life. Being promoted to assistant manager at the store where she worked made it possible to meet her expenses without having to depend on anyone else. For the first time ever she had her very own place, where her siblings couldn't find her and move themselves in, taking everything from her that she didn't have bolted down—including her dignity and self-respect.

Everything had been going fine until she'd stopped by her mother's house last week to see how she was doing. As always, Thelma had asked her to help go over the bills. In the middle of it, Melody's younger sister, Lydia, started begging for a ride. Melody finally gave in, only because their mother had insisted. But after she'd dropped Lydia off, Melody realized that all the money in her purse was gone. She'd gone back to her mother's to finish going over the bills, trying not to feel angry, trying not to take it out on her mother. She reminded herself that Thelma Morgan was a victim, just like the rest of them. She had spent most of her life married to an alcoholic who had raged and controlled his wife and children. He had died a few years earlier, which had come as a relief to everyone who knew him. But Roy Morgan's sons had quickly taken over his role, barely hanging on to a job here and there, drinking themselves into oblivion at every possible opportunity. And Thelma's senses had been dulled over the years by oppression and intimidation. She didn't know how to do anything but try to keep her grown children from complaining.

As they finished sorting out the bills, Melody firmly declared, "If you would stop dishing out money to the kids, you'd have enough to make ends meet, Mom. You're going to have to keep track of the bills and stay on top of them. I'm not going to do it for you anymore."

Thelma said nothing.

"Mother? Are you hearing what I'm telling you?"

"Yes, dear," she said as if she was a child being scolded.

Melody was getting ready to leave when she realized that her brother, Joe, had just driven off in her car. She knew he was drunk, and in spite of her mother's protests, she called the police. She reported the car stolen and Joe was arrested. But not before he drove the car into a garbage dumpster and totaled it. Melody was grateful he hadn't killed somebody; but she still didn't have a car. And she didn't have any money until payday—all thanks to her family.

Now, as she approached the front door of her mother's home, Melody steeled herself for the inevitable onslaught. Reminding herself not to be intimidated, she quickly thought through everything she'd learned about breaking codependency. Then she walked in. The usual stale aromas assaulted her; the most prevalent being the cigarette smoke. Her oldest brother, Ben, was passed out on the couch, snoring loudly. Snoring was better than yelling and swearing. That was one good thing. Joe was still in jail. That was another positive note.

Melody found her mother in bed, half asleep. "Hi, Mom," she said and Thelma looked up with red eyes. "It's past noon. Are you sick?"

"No, I just . . ."

"Taking Valium again?"

"Only once in a while, dear. What are you doing here? I didn't expect to ever see you again after what Joe did, and—"

"That has nothing to do with you, Mother." Melody started picking up clothes off the floor, if only to keep herself from thinking too hard. Trying to distinguish the clean from the dirty, she said, "I told Lydia I was coming. Where is she?"

"She left about an hour ago, I think."

Melody barely stopped herself from cussing out loud. It was a habit she'd found difficult to break, in light of the fact that her entire family cussed more than they blinked.

"She told me she'd be here," Melody protested. "She promised she'd have some of the money she owes me. Oooh!" Melody angrily tossed a handful of dirty clothes into the overflowing hamper.

"Lydia's having a hard time, dear," Thelma reminded her.

"Yes, I know. She's seventeen and pregnant. I know, Mother. I know. Does that make it all right for her to steal money out of my purse, and lie to me, and—"

"No, of course not," Thelma said in a tone of voice that indicated she was tuning Melody out.

"I don't suppose you have a few dollars you could loan me until I get paid?"

"I'm sorry, dear, but I gave it to—"

"I don't even want to know," Melody interrupted.

"I tried to call you, but the recording said your number had been changed."

"That's right."

"You told me you were moving, but shouldn't you have the same phone number if—"

"I had the number changed, Mother. I explained it all to you the last time I was here."

Melody glanced at her watch. If she couldn't get any money for bus fare, she'd have to leave now or she'd never make it to her appointment. "I don't suppose you've heard from Lisa," she said. Since the remainder of her day would be spent covering for her older sister's negligence, she had to ask.

"Not since she called to tell me she'd made it to Mexico."

"Mexico," Melody mumbled under her breath.

"What was that?" Thelma asked.

"I was just wondering if she'd by any chance miraculously sent any portion of the several hundred dollars she owes me."

"Haven't seen anything," Thelma said, then she yawned.

"I have to go, Mother. I'll try to keep in touch."

Melody hurried out of the house, feeling as if just being there would suffocate her. She reminded herself that she had done everything in her power to help her family, and her efforts had gotten her nothing but heartache. She had learned a long time ago that she could do nothing to help her siblings; and the only thing she could do for her mother was to be independent enough that she wasn't one more burden on Thelma's Social Security check. But once in a while, Melody just got feeling sorry for them, and inevitably she'd get sucked back into their problems. It was as if the family was some kind of enormous vacuum, pulling her into a downward spiral, draining everything good out of her.

Melody fastened her old coat around her, tightened the scarf around her ears, and began walking briskly toward downtown Provo. Occasionally she pulled her hand out of its warm pocket to check her watch. If she kept a good pace, she might actually make it. Being late would be just what she needed; *failure to appear in court* on top of everything else. At the moment she didn't feel the least bit sorry for her siblings. If she saw any one of them right now, she'd be tempted to physically strangle them.

She thought back to her high school graduation. She was the only one in the family who had made it that far, but her mother hadn't come to the ceremony, and her father had died that year. Melody had immediately gone out to look for a job, and found an apartment as soon as she could afford it. But her older sister, Lisa, had moved in with her—against Melody's wishes. Lisa had caused a number of problems, including some damages to the apartment that Melody was being sued for. She had tried every possible avenue to get it taken care of, but now it would go before a judge, and she knew the outcome was inevitable. And, of course, Lisa was nowhere around. She'd gone to Mexico with her latest live-in boyfriend; this went along with her recent anti-patriotism, since the government had taken her illegitimate children away when she neglected them.

Knowing anger wouldn't get her anywhere, Melody prayed inwardly for the strength to forgive and be free of this heartache. She prayed to be able to make it through the day. Walking down University Avenue, she noticed the city Christmas decorations being put up. As always, evidence of the holidays made all that was bad seem even worse.

By the time she got to the courthouse, Melody was hungry and exhausted. She had to run the last two blocks, and she came into the building with her lungs burning from the cold. She hurried to the appointed courtroom, praying that they were sufficiently behind schedule to give her a chance to catch her breath. As it turned out, they were so far behind that she became infuriated at having hurried so fast. Her stomach growled, and she wished she'd packed herself a lunch this morning. She rummaged in her purse, hoping to find fifty cents that she could use in a vending machine, but there was nothing beyond a few pennies.

Resigning herself to just getting this over with, Melody glanced around. Even the courthouse had signs of Christmas; they were everywhere she turned. Her reasons for hating Christmas inevitably took her thoughts back to where they had started. It seemed that no matter how hard she tried to live right and be a good person, her family and upbringing plagued her like an enormous ball and chain around her ankle.

Melody was startled when her name was called. She took a deep breath and reminded herself to maintain her dignity, no matter what happened. She only prayed the judge would be compassionate.

As the facts were laid out, Melody felt that ball and chain tightening around her ankle. At moments like this she could almost wish she'd never been born. She couldn't wait to get out of here, but then she'd just have to walk home in the cold. *Please, dear Father,* she prayed in her mind, *just help me get through this day.*

Chapter Two

Melody fought back the tears pounding in her head as the judge delivered his verdict. She reminded herself that she was not a criminal, and his attitude toward her certainly didn't imply that she was. But the whole situation was simply too familiar. It seemed to be the story of her life: no matter how hard she tried to do the right thing, she always got stuck innocently holding the bag. And she felt just plain weary.

She managed a nod to indicate she was listening as the judge explained, "I understand this is difficult for you, Miss Morgan. But seeing that it is your signature on the apartment lease, I have no choice but to hold you accountable for the damages done by your sister." Melody sighed and forced back her emotion. As the judge continued with some words of advice in a firm voice, she wondered if she would ever be able to just live a calm, normal life.

Melody began to wish this would just end. If she had to hold her emotion in check for even another thirty seconds, exhausted and hungry as she was, she felt certain she would pass out. The moment she was excused, she turned to leave and the tears spilled. Paying no attention to anyone or anything, she rushed out of the room and down the hall. She couldn't get out of here fast enough.

In the flurry of her escape, she collided with a stout woman who carried an enormous handbag. The contents of Melody's purse scattered across the floor as she barely managed to keep from falling flat on her face. The woman huffed past, her irritation obvious. Melody resisted the urge to swear at her and frantically struggled to gather her things. She cursed herself inwardly for being the kind of woman who had to carry everything with her for every possible emergency. And she couldn't believe how many of her possessions were round, rolling away from her in every direction. As people rushed past, paying no heed to her beyond their irritation at having to dodge the objects on the floor, Melody wondered if there was any goodness at all left in the world. She was nearly ready to abandon her belongings and run. Just then, a masculine hand picked up her lipstick and a bottle of Tylenol, stuffing them nonchalantly into her open purse.

Melody paused briefly to take a sidelong glance at his white shirt and navy blue tie, suspenders, dark slacks, and a head of sandy-blond hair that waved back off his brow, then tightened into a mass of loose, lush curls. She hurried to grab the few remaining items, embarrassed to realize that there were feminine products among them. "Thank you," she said, wishing it hadn't sounded so terse as she stood up and quickly slung her purse over her shoulder. She caught her breath unexpectedly when the man who had helped her stood up straight, holding out a pack of gum and a tiny bottle of hair spray. She absently took them and looked up to meet his eyes; dark blue eyes, she noticed. *He was so tall.*

Clearing her throat in an attempt to clear her head, Melody glanced down and stuffed the gum and hair spray into her purse. She was five foot eight herself, so most men were usually pretty close to eye level. But rather than feeling intimidated by this man's height, she felt somehow warmed by his simple act of kindness. She wanted to tell him he'd given her a glimmer of hope that the world was not a completely rotten place, but she settled for a simple "Thank you" and walked away.

"Wait," he said, following after her. Melody kept walking. "Are you okay?"

"I'm fine, thank you," she said, wondering why on earth he would care.

"I . . . was just wondering," he rambled as they stepped out into the bitter air and Melody pulled her coat tightly around her. "I mean . . . I just got the impression that you weren't having a good day."

Melody stopped on the courthouse steps and turned to look at him. "Whatever gave you that idea?" she asked in a voice dripping with sarcasm.

He shrugged his shoulders and smiled. She knew his type. There was something intangible about him that made her certain he'd grown up with everything he'd ever needed—or wanted. He probably had parents who had taken him to church and actually taught him the difference between right and wrong. He'd probably never gone hungry a day in his life, and had no idea what reality was like. She couldn't help her sharp tone as she asked, "Do I know you?"

"Not yet," he said with a confidence that should have been arrogant, but wasn't.

Melody scrutinized him once again. For a moment she indulged in a fantasy, considering the possibility that a man like this would actually find a long-term interest in a woman like her. But it only took a moment to come to a firm conclusion. She knew from experience that people from different sides of the tracks—whether figurative or literal—just didn't make it together in this world. That kind of thing only happened in fairy tales, and she had stopped believing in fairy tales at the age of four. While it was tempting to indulge herself in this man's attention—however brief it might be—she felt certain that it wouldn't be worth the inevitable pain when he found out what kind of woman she really was.

"I need to go," she said, moving on down the stairs. "It's cold."

"Where's your car parked?" he asked.

"What difference does it make?" she snapped and kept walking.

"I just wanted to know," he stated.

"Listen," she stopped and faced him, "I *have* had a bad day, and I don't need any more interference right now."

He looked momentarily so deflated that she almost wanted to take back her clipped words.

"I'm sorry," he said. "It's just that . . . I was in the courtroom, and . . . I thought the verdict was a little harsh. I mean . . . I guess it's just one of those things, but . . . ."

Matthew Trevor looked into this woman's eyes and forced himself to stop stammering. How could he possibly explain the way he'd felt as he listened to her explanations in the courtroom? Or the way those feelings had deepened when she'd walked past him, carrying herself with a dignity that completely defied the tears streaming down her face? He'd followed her on impulse, and now he felt almost desperate to not let her out of his sight. He'd always been taught to trust his instincts; to listen to the Spirit and never ignore its promptings. He'd learned to practice the theory nearly every day through the course of his mission. But he wondered if he'd ever felt so strongly about *anything* as he felt standing here right now. He just didn't know how to tell *her* his feelings without sounding like an utter fool.

"What I'm trying to say, Miss Morgan, is that I hope your day gets better. And, well . . . what I really want to know is . . . well, is there anything I can do to help?"

Melody sighed. "You're joking, right?"

"No," he insisted, looking insulted at the suggestion.

Melody attempted to come up with a good reason not to trust this man. Any excuse at all to just walk away and pass the incident off. But the man was standing there freezing, looking as if his world might end if she didn't talk to him. She couldn't recall ever seeing such genuine emotion in *anyone.*

"How do I know you're not some con artist or rapist or something?"

His laughter was so genuine that she couldn't help laughing, too.

"Miss Morgan," he said, "I was just wondering if I could buy you some dinner. If you don't want to go, just say so. We can walk right over there." He pointed to the little Mexican restaurant across the street. "And we can stay in public."

Melody looked at the restaurant. She loved that place. And she couldn't remember the last time she'd gone out to eat. It was cold. It was almost dark. She was *starving*. And this guy—whoever he might be—was simply adorable. She quickly gauged her instincts and couldn't think of any reason to protest.

It was only a meal, she thought, reminding herself that she needed to be more trusting. Only a few minutes ago she had been thinking that he'd restored her faith in the goodness of mankind. Now she was trying to denounce his efforts.

"Okay," she said, "but I think you'd better get your coat. You're turning blue."

Matthew grinned. "I'll just be a minute. Maybe you should wait inside."

Melody nodded and followed him back through the door. He took a few steps and turned back. "You won't leave?" he asked.

Melody held up her arms dramatically. "I'll wait right here. I promise." He arched one eyebrow as if to question *her* motives. She added with a little laugh, "I love that restaurant."

Matthew grabbed his coat and briefcase just as the courtroom was being closed up for the night. He nearly ran back to the door where he'd left her waiting. His heart quickened when he saw her, and he found it strange that he recalled hearing his father tell him that the first time he'd laid eyes on his mother, he knew she would be a significant part of his life. He quickly squelched the idea, convinced that he was letting his thoughts get out of hand. But when she saw him and smiled, something tingled down his arms.

"See, I didn't run away," she said. "I'm a woman of my word."

They walked outside together. "Is that why having to pay for someone else's negligence is so difficult?" he asked.

Melody was so surprised by the question that she nearly slipped at the bottom of the stairs. He grabbed her arm and saved her. "You okay?" he asked, letting go as she steadied herself.

"Yes, thank you. It would seem you've saved me twice now."

"You didn't answer my question," he said as they waited at the corner for the light to turn.

Melody sighed, hoping to avoid it. "Paying for

someone else's negligence is the story of my life." Matthew wanted to ask what she meant by that, but she said, "I don't even know your name."

"Matthew Trevor," he said, holding out his hand.

She shook it tentatively and they started across the road while the *walk* signal chirped like some kind of mechanical bird.

"Melody Morgan," she replied. Then recalling that he'd been in the courtroom, she added, "But you already knew that."

They walked into the restaurant and were seated before anything more was said. "So, Mr. Trevor, you know why *I* was in court today, but you haven't told me what *you* were doing there. Auto theft? Armed robbery? Homicide?"

Matthew laughed. "Nothing so exciting, I'm afraid. Actually, I'm a law student. I enjoy hanging out in courtrooms."

She gave him a sidelong glance, saying, "You need to get out more, Mr. Trevor."

Matthew smiled. He liked her sense of humor. But he had to admit, "Yes, I'm certain you're right. It's been a long time since I've sat across a table from a woman . . . except for my mother and sisters, that is."

"And why is that?"

"I haven't found a woman who could lure me away from the courtroom."

He said it lightly, but Melody saw something in his eyes that made her pulse quicken. His implication was something she wanted to savor, and at the same time run away from.

"Well," she said, forcing herself to look elsewhere, "I still can't figure why I'm sitting here with *you*. I'm not prone to going out with someone I've never laid eyes on."

"Well, that makes two of us," he said. "So, now that we're together, maybe we should get to know each other a little better. Are you from around here, Melody?" He added as an afterthought, "May I call you Melody?"

"Sure," she said, but the last thing she wanted was to talk about herself. "I grew up in Provo, yes," she answered, and left it at that.

"And your family?"

Melody sighed. "Oh, they're around. How about you?"

"Oh, I've lived in Provo most of my life. I'm living with my parents for the time being. I'd like to get through school with as little debt as possible. It's nice to grow up in a college town, for that reason. I'm the oldest by a significant span of years, so the rest are quite a bit younger."

"The rest?"

"Two sisters. Caitlin is fourteen, and Mallory is thirteen. And two brothers. Jake is seven, and Dustin is five."

"Wow, that is quite a spread," she said, and continued to ask him questions. Over their meal she verified what she had already guessed. He obviously came from a good family, and he'd lived a good life. He was following in his father's footsteps by choosing a career in law.

"Not that he forced it or anything," Matthew clarified. "It's just that I always admired what he did. His work always really meant something to him."

Melody managed to ask questions and keep Matthew talking about himself through the entire meal—which kept them from talking about her. She discovered that he'd gone on a mission to Russia. He worked at a sporting goods store, and served in the Young Men's organization in his ward.

"So you're a Mormon," she said.

Matthew was startled. When he'd acted on his

impulses to meet her, he'd never even considered that she might not be a member of the Church. "Yes," he said without apologizing.

"Well, I'll chalk that up as one point in your favor," she said, and he smiled. "I was teaching Primary before I moved recently. Seven-year-olds." He nodded and she urged the conversation back to him. "So what do you do in your free time?" She'd meant it as a joke, knowing he had to be incredibly busy.

But Matthew responded quickly, "I volunteer time at a local crisis center."

"Why?" she asked, wishing it hadn't sounded so incredulous.

"Why not?" he replied.

"I mean . . . I think it's great. It's just that you must be awfully busy—working, a church job, going to law school. I just thought people who did that kind of thing were bored and unfulfilled. You don't seem to have those qualifications."

Matthew laughed.

"Is it funny?"

"You just have a way of putting things that . . . well, I like it." Melody said nothing, and he went on to answer her question. "I can't say my life is boring, but perhaps a little unfulfilling at this point. I really don't put much time in at the crisis center these days, but when I do, I enjoy it. I got into it because my mother has done it off and on for years."

"Is she bored and unfulfilled?"

"Not hardly," he said lightly.

"Well," Melody said with subtle drama, "I guess that teaches me something about judging people. I'll have to rethink my expectations of people who are bored and unfulfilled."

"Are *you* bored and unfulfilled?" Matthew asked, his tone becoming more serious.

Melody glanced away. "Maybe I am. Well, not bored . . . but possibly unfulfilled."

"We could maybe do something about that."

"What?" she laughed. "Put me to work at a crisis center?"

"Maybe."

"I don't think so," she insisted, avoiding the fact that she was related to a number of people who could probably use a great deal of help from a crisis center. It seemed her family was always in a crisis of one kind or another.

She was relieved when Matthew didn't press the issue. Instead he asked, "So what do *you* do with your free time?"

"I'm an assistant manager at Blockbuster Video. I'd like to take some classes next semester, but for the moment my resources are a bit limited. When I do get back to school, I want to get a degree in elementary education. But right now, I just work. That's all."

Since they'd finished their meal, Melody was able to evade any more questions. As they stepped outside, she noticed again the evidence of Christmas decorations going up. She sighed, wondering what it might be like to actually anticipate a holiday, or to have fond memories of Christmases gone by. As it was, Christmas and everything related to it only spurred a formless ache inside her. So she did her best to ignore it.

"I wonder if it will ever snow this year," Matthew said, buttoning his long, navy-colored wool coat.

"Who knows?" she said.

"Well, I hope it snows before Christmas. It just doesn't seem right without snow."

"Actually, I hate snow," she said. He looked mildly alarmed but said nothing more about it.

"So, where's your car?" he asked. "I'll walk you to it."

"No, that's okay," she insisted. "I can take care of myself, I assure you, Mr. Trevor."

"My name is Matthew. And I'm certain you can take care of yourself. But my mother taught me to be a gentleman—and that means escorting a lady to her car."

When it became evident that he would not let up, Melody had to admit, "I don't have a car at the moment."

"How did you get here?"

"I walked."

"Okay then, I'll drive you home."

"You're not going to leave me in peace, are you."

"Not unless you're really mean to me. I can take a hint eventually. But right now, I'm going to take you home."

Matthew took Melody's hand without her permission and walked back toward the courthouse parking lot. He unlocked the door of a little blue convertible and held it open for her. She couldn't help thinking of the contrast to her own car—the one she didn't have anymore.

As if Matthew had read her mind, he got into the car, asking, "What's wrong with your car?"

Melody sighed. It would be a lot easier if she believed in lying. But growing up as she had, where the lines between truth and lies had been so difficult to define, she had taught herself to be adamantly honest. At times it was the only thing that could make her feel like she had risen above the Morgan mentality.

"My brother borrowed it and got in an accident. The car is totaled."

"Is your brother all right?" he asked with concern.

"He's fine," she stated, looking out the window.

Matthew backed out of the parking space. "Where do you live?"

She told him the address and he growled, "You walked all the way from there—in this cold?"

"Actually, I walked from my mother's, which is a little further—in the other direction," she said without apology. She didn't add that until she got paid again, she couldn't even come up with the change for a bus fare.

"Why?" he demanded as if he had a right to know.

"Mr. Trevor," she said indignantly, "since the chance of our seeing each other again is extremely remote, I don't see what difference it makes."

"It makes a difference to *me,*" he said. "And to be quite honest, I had every hope of seeing you again—soon."

"Why?" she demanded in the same tone he'd used with her.

"Because I like you," he insisted.

Melody just chuckled and looked out the window. *If he only knew,* she thought.

For all his efforts, Matthew wasn't able to provoke any more conversation with her beyond the weather and himself. He walked her to the door of her basement apartment, but she stopped a few feet away from the door, saying firmly, "Thank you, Mr. Trevor. You've been very kind."

"May I call you?" he asked.

"You're wasting your time," she insisted.

Matthew scowled. "You have a boyfriend, don't you."

Melody sighed and simply stated, "Good night, Mr. Trevor."

"My name is Matthew," he insisted, but she only slammed the door.

Chapter Three

For three days, Matthew couldn't force thoughts of Melody Morgan out of his head. He was grateful to have his studies well under control when it became practically impossible to concentrate. He even prayed about it, and he couldn't deny the feeling that he needed to find her. It remained to be seen if his romantic interest in her would ever come to anything. Either way, he just knew he had to follow these feelings.

The minute Matthew got home from his classes, he went to the phone book.

"What are you looking for?" his mother asked as she leaned against the counter, wiping her hands on a towel.

"Oh hi, Mom," he said, pressing a kiss to her cheek. Then he answered her question as he flipped through the Yellow Pages. "Blockbuster Video."

"You need to rent something?"

"Not exactly," he said, startled to realize how many Blockbuster Video stores there were in Utah Valley. He took the phone book to the family room where he could have privacy, and started at the top of the list, simply asking if Melody was in. After being told several times that he had the wrong number, he heard the voice on the other end of the phone say, "Oh, she'll be here in about an hour."

Matthew wondered if it was possible there could be another Melody who worked at Blockbuster Video. To reassure himself, he called the rest of the stores on the list. Sure enough, there was only one.

Matthew returned the phone book, telling his mother, "I'm going out for a while."

"What's up?" she asked.

"I'm just going to Blockbuster."

"But *not exactly* to rent a video?" she questioned with a little smile.

"That's right," he chuckled.

Her expression made it clear that she wouldn't press him, but she was dying of curiosity. Before he could tell her she guessed, "It's a girl, right?"

Matthew chuckled again. "That's right. It's a girl."

"Good luck," she said.

Recalling Melody's attitude toward him, Matthew muttered under his breath, "I'm going to need it."

Walking into the store, he felt a sudden rush of nerves. He wandered around nonchalantly once he realized that she wasn't at the front desk. He was just beginning to wonder if he might have the wrong Melody when he saw her on the *Adventure* aisle, putting video tapes away. His nerves suddenly turned to butterflies. He felt like a school kid going to his first dance as he stepped toward her.

"Excuse me," he said, "could you tell me where I might find some adventure?"

Melody looked up and attempted to ignore the quickening of her heart. Matthew Trevor was the last person she'd expected to see here. But she didn't want to admit that she'd thought of little else besides him the past few days.

"What are you doing here?" she snapped, if only to cover what his nearness did to her. She'd never felt this way in her life—and it scared her.

"I was looking for adventure," he said, motioning to the little sign. "It says this is the Adventure section."

Melody uttered a sigh of disgust, then she couldn't help laughing. "How did you find me?"

"It wasn't easy. I had to fight off a man-eating crocodile and cross a scorpion-infested desert, but . . . I'm here!"

"How tender," she said with light sarcasm. "How did you *really* find me?"

"The Yellow Pages. Do you know how many Blockbusters there are in this valley?"

"Yes," she drawled. "And . . ."

"Okay, so I'll get to the point."

"I wish you would."

"Hey," he lowered his voice, "would you go out with me?"

"I already did."

"Again, I mean."

"I don't get off until midnight," she insisted.

"And tomorrow?"

"I work the same shift tomorrow."

"A girl so adorable should not be working the Friday evening shift." She scowled at him and he added, "How about Saturday?"

Melody wanted to tell him to mind his own business, but she couldn't think of one good reason to send him away—beyond an indescribable fear that was in itself somehow compelling. What was she afraid of? Having him find out the truth about her and leave her high and dry?

Or getting her heart involved before he did? Maybe it was already too late on that last count.

"What did you have in mind?" she asked, and he grinned.

"I need to go Christmas shopping," he said. "And I hate going alone."

Melody wrinkled her nose, wanting to tell him she had no desire to do *anything* related to Christmas. "It's not even Thanksgiving yet," she protested.

"Oh, I like to get an early start. Then I thought we could do dinner and a movie."

Melody heard herself say "Okay" before she hardly thought about it. Matthew grinned as if she'd just handed him the world on a silver platter. She couldn't figure why he'd feel that way, but she decided to enjoy it while it lasted. If nothing else, he was offering some free meals and recreation. And with her financial situation, free was great.

"I'll pick you up Saturday about one," he said and she nodded.

Not wanting to leave, he asked, "So did you get a car yet?"

"Not yet," she said, concentrating on her work with the hope that he wouldn't press her with questions.

"How did you get here?"

"I walked." She scowled and added firmly, "And please don't ask me *why*. I'll see you Saturday."

Matthew left while he was ahead, but he was waiting outside the video store when she walked out soon after midnight. She looked surprised but said little as she got in the car and he drove toward her apartment. Matthew did most of the talking, if only to ease the silence. She thanked him when she got out, and the following evening he showed up at midnight again to take her home.

"I thought you were a busy man," she said.

"I am."

"So, why are you—"

"Don't ask me why, Melody. Because I'm not certain that I'm ready to answer that yet."

She looked alarmed. "Why?"

He laughed and said, "I'm not answering that, either."

"Why?"

"You don't answer my questions. Why should I answer yours?"

She looked mildly disgusted and said nothing more beyond thanking him for the ride when she got out of the car.

He picked her up Saturday at one o'clock as he'd promised. She was kind and polite, but he sensed that she was extremely uncomfortable. They went to the mall and wandered slowly down the long corridors, while he held her hand possessively. After an hour of browsing, during which Matthew did most of the talking, he finally just asked, "Is something bothering you?" She looked alarmed and he added, "Listen, I know I've been a little pushy, and I have absolutely no idea whether you even like me or not. If you really don't want to be here, just say so."

"Oh, no," Melody insisted, "it's not that at all. I just . . ." She didn't know how to explain without sounding like an idiot.

"You just what?" he asked. When she only glanced away, he led her to a bench and urged her to sit down. Sitting to face her, he said gently, "Listen, Melody, it's difficult for me to explain why I have this irresistible urge to just be with you. I don't know what it means. And I'm not trying to propose or anything. But I do believe in being completely honest. All I ask is that you do the same. Do you have a problem with that?"

Melody shook her head slowly. She wasn't certain how to react to a man who was demanding honesty right up front.

"Okay," he went on, "so maybe we should talk. Or would you prefer that I just take you home?"

Melody said nothing, but she found it difficult to take her eyes from his.

"Well?" he laughed, albeit tensely.

She glanced down and chuckled. "I'm sorry. It's just that I've never . . . dated anyone like you before. I'm not sure if I . . ."

"What?" he urged, gently taking her hand.

Melody wondered how to explain. "You'll have to be patient with me, Matthew. Communication and honesty were not really strong parts of my upbringing. It isn't easy for me to talk to somebody who actually wants to talk."

Melody expected him to seem uncomfortable with the information she'd just given him, however minimal. But he relaxed and became more attentive, as if he had all the time in the world.

Following an excruciating silence, he said, "I'm still waiting."

"I don't know what to say."

"I just need to know whether or not you want me to take you home."

"No, of course not." How could she possibly deny the pleasure she found in his presence?

"Okay, we're narrowing it down. Are you uncomfortable with me, or—"

"Yes," she admitted, and his obvious concern made her wonder if this communication thing was such a good idea. She hurried to add, "But not for the reasons you might think."

"And for what reasons do I make you uncomfortable?" he asked in a way that made it easy for her to imagine him being a lawyer.

Inspired by his forthright nature, Melody squared her shoulders and looked him in the eye, admitting in a soft voice, "Because no one has ever made me feel the way you do."

Matthew was so relieved he couldn't hold back a delighted little laugh. When Melody only glanced away, he clarified, "And that's why you feel uncomfortable with me?"

Melody didn't know how to explain her fear that getting emotionally involved with him would just lead to heartache, so she simply said, "I'm more uncomfortable with . . . the activity." He looked confused and she said, "I hate Christmas shopping."

Matthew laughed again.

"Is that funny?"

He shook his head. "It's just that . . . I asked my mother what she thought a woman would like to do, and she said women like to shop. I'm sorry. I should have asked *you.*"

"Oh, I don't mind shopping, really . . . window shopping at least."

"But you just said that—"

"I said that I hate *Christmas* shopping." She was not only serious, she was vehement.

"Why?" he asked.

Melody contemplated a number of responses, but there was only one completely honest answer. "I've just always had a hard time with Christmas. I'm afraid I'm kind of a Scrooge."

"Well, shame on you," he smirked, but his light attitude helped her feel a little better. "No, seriously," he leaned a little closer, "if you don't want to go shopping, we'll do something else. We can hit a matinee movie, or—"

"It's okay," she said. "I think I feel better just knowing I don't have to pretend that I like Christmas shopping."

"All right," he stood with her hand in his, "we'll make a few stops, just enough to say I got started, then we'll go somewhere else."

"Okay," she agreed.

Melody relaxed as she concentrated on Matthew Trevor's company and ignored the presence of Christmas decor and music. She couldn't help being in awe of his character, his personality, his insistence in making her talk. She had simply never considered that someone like him might exist. Besides, her fear of becoming emotionally involved was irrelevant and she knew it. She was already sunk. If she never saw Matthew Trevor again, she knew her heart would break.

While Matthew had felt it was important not to make a big issue of Melody's aversion to Christmas, he couldn't help wondering what was behind her guarded nature. He wanted to ask her, but they hardly knew each other. Perhaps with time, and a little divine intervention, he could eventually get to know the *real* Melody Morgan. It was something he could spend his entire life doing, he decided as he watched her try perfume samples on her arm at the ZCMI cosmetics counter. She declared she didn't like any of them, so they went to the housewares department instead, searching for a gift for his mother.

"What's she like, your mother?" Melody asked as she stood a step above him on the escalator.

Matthew erupted with a delighted little laugh that she realized was common for him. He said with pleasure, "My mother is incredible."

"I don't know why that doesn't surprise me," she said.

"And why is that?"

Melody prompted herself to honesty. "She has an incredible son."

"I'll take that as a compliment," he said as they stepped off the escalator.

While they were looking at kitchen paraphernalia, Matthew felt prompted to share a thought that wouldn't leave his mind. "I'll tell you what my mother is like. She's like you in twenty years."

Melody looked up at him in surprise, wondering what he meant. He touched her nose with his finger and said, "You don't have to understand that. Just take it as a compliment."

Matthew settled on buying his mother a cookie jar that looked like a rooster. When the head was lifted to get inside, it crowed. He laughed as he tried it over and over, drawing the attention of everyone standing nearby. "She will *love* this," he said, carrying it to the checkout counter.

"And why is that?" Melody asked.

"I have two little brothers who have been affectionately dubbed 'the cookie snitchers'."

With a purchase made, Matthew declared that since his Christmas shopping was officially *started,* they could go now. They went to an early movie, then he took her to dinner. Over their meal, Matthew asked, "So, have you got something to drive yet?"

"No," she said, not wanting to talk about this.

"Why not? You can't walk everywhere you go in this weather."

"I can take the bus," she insisted.

"But you don't," he stated while his eyes delved into hers, seeming to ask what was obvious.

Melody sighed. "What are you trying to do to me? Is it really so important that you know every little detail of my life?"

"Not yet," he said with a confidence that almost infuriated her. He leaned closer and softened his voice. "Believe it or not, Melody, I'm concerned about you."

"What is there to be worried about?" she retorted, trying not to get angry.

"A woman walking home in sub-zero temperatures after dark, for one. Whatever you were slapped with in court is another. I don't recall the details of the problem, but I know you got left holding something that you shouldn't have been holding. Am I looking at a woman who doesn't like to go Christmas shopping because she can't even afford a bus fare?"

Melody attempted to stare him down, but he won and she looked away.

"If I'm assuming wrongly, Melody, feel free to straighten me out. If you don't want to talk to me about it, I guess that's up to you. But God didn't put us on this earth to solve all of our problems alone. If there's something I can do to help, it would be a pleasure, I can assure you."

"There's nothing anybody can do to help, Matthew," she snapped. "I am quite accustomed to taking care of myself."

"Not having a means to get to work is not taking care of yourself."

Melody's anger rose as she snarled quietly, "You have no idea what you're talking about, *Mr. Trevor*. How could you possibly know what makes me do what I do?"

"I can't if you don't tell me," he stated calmly.

"Well, it's none of your business. You have no idea what the *real* world is like. So why don't you just go back to your posh little life and leave me alone?"

While Matthew was trying to figure exactly what she was accusing him of, she got up and left the table. He assumed that she'd gone to the ladies' room, but when she didn't come back he realized that she had left the restaurant. He looked at her half-eaten meal and wished he'd just kept his mouth shut. Now she was walking home, cold *and* hungry. As he stood up and pulled his wallet out to leave a tip, he noticed her purse sitting on the seat. He picked it up and paid for the meal, then hurried out to the car, trying to figure which direction she'd gone. He uttered a quick prayer, then felt compelled to look in her wallet. He found nothing beyond a library card and a driver's license. No credit cards. No money beyond a few pennies—literally. Matthew impulsively put a twenty-dollar bill in her wallet, then he glanced closer at her driver's license before he put it back. *Melody Noel Morgan.* "A Christmas baby," he said aloud, glancing at her birth date. *December 21.* He found her declaration of disliking Christmas ironic.

Matthew drove only a few blocks before he found her, walking briskly, obviously freezing. He pulled the car up beside her and reached over to open the passenger door. She stared at him until he hollered, "If you never want to see me again, fine. But get in before you freeze to death." She still didn't move and he held up her purse. "You forgot this. If you want it back, you're going to have to get in the car."

Melody got in and slammed the door. Not knowing whether to feel touched by his concern, angry at his arrogance, or humiliated that he had figured out her life was a mess, Melody simply said nothing as he drove.

When they were almost to her apartment, Matthew said gently, "Forgive me, Melody, for being less than tactful. I realize you don't know me very well, and there's probably no good reason for you to trust me. I'm just . . . concerned." He glanced at her briefly then turned his eyes back to the road. "Just don't be so proud that you go without, Melody. You have the gospel. Use it."

She said nothing as he stopped the car. Their eyes met briefly before she got out, saying only, "Thanks for the ride."

Melody lay awake half the night, trying to figure out what was going on between her heart and her head. No matter how she tried, she couldn't free her thoughts of Matthew Trevor. And at the same time, she wondered how to deal with the financial nightmare hanging over her head. She kept hearing Matthew's voice telling her not to go without because of pride. She prayed to understand, but she didn't see how pride had anything to do with it. What was Matthew going to do? Buy her a car and pay her bills? She wouldn't want him to, even if he could afford it. They hardly knew each other, for crying out loud. But then her thoughts drifted back to their meeting at the courthouse. Hadn't she been praying for a way to make it through the day? Hadn't he helped her out of an embarrassing situation? Provided her with a good meal? Given her a ride home? And he'd been her transportation twice since, when it had been dark and cold. Was Matthew Trevor the answer to her prayers, and was she simply too proud to accept it?

The pride thing was still hovering uneasily in Melody's conscience the next morning when she went to Relief Society. The lesson was on bearing one another's burdens, with a great deal of emphasis on the need for those who are struggling to allow others to help them. As the lesson began to strike too close to sensitive issues, Melody rummaged quietly through her purse, if only to keep her hands busy. Opening her wallet, she gasped softly, briefly drawing the attention of the woman sitting at her side. At first she wondered if she had simply overlooked the fact that she had twenty dollars. But she knew how hard and deep she had searched for any hidden money the last several days. It took about a second to figure out the only possible conclusion. She'd left her purse at the restaurant, and Matthew had given it back to her when he'd picked her up. At first she considered every possible means of giving it back to him, letting him know with all of the indignation she felt that she had no intention of becoming some charity case to him. Then her ear tuned back into the lesson, and Matthew Trevor's words echoed through her mind. *Just don't be so proud that you go without, Melody. You have the gospel. Use it.*

Melody made an appointment with her bishop that evening and explained the circumstances. He showed a great deal of compassion, and they talked about ways she could let her family know of her love for them without allowing them to take advantage of her. She was given a check to cover the apartment damages her sister had left on her shoulders, and enough for a down payment on a car, in addition to a little extra to tide her over for the few days until she got a paycheck. The bishop also offered to call her insurance company and see if he could help straighten out the mess created by her brother's accident—something she'd been avoiding because she simply didn't know how to handle it.

Together they went over a plan for her to repay some of the money by working at the bishop's storehouse; the remainder would be paid back with fast offering donations. Melody came away feeling extremely humbled and blessed. And not the least bit humiliated. Her bishop had shown no judgment toward her, and by giving her the opportunity to work off the help he'd given her, she didn't feel like a charity case.

Melody felt better as she took a bus to work the next morning. About an hour after she got there, a bouquet of flowers was delivered for her. No one had *ever* sent her flowers. The card read simply, "I'm thinking about you, Matthew." She unconsciously put a hand to her heart as it quickened at the thought of him. Maybe he really was the blessing that he appeared to be. Maybe she just needed to get past her pride and fears and enjoy his friendship, without worrying too much about the future.

Chapter Four

Matthew found it difficult to concentrate in his classes and as he studied through the afternoon. He went to work in the evening, his mind so consumed with Melody Morgan that he could hardly think straight. He was arranging a Christmas display of mountain-climbing equipment when a feminine voice said, "Could you tell me where I might find some adventure?"

Matthew smiled before he turned to look at Melody. "How on earth did you find me?" he asked.

"The Yellow Pages," she replied. "Do you know how many sporting goods stores there are in this valley? There's a Matthew who works in that one by the mall, but he was short and bald." She smiled and added, "I don't think he's the one who sent me flowers."

Matthew only shrugged. He was so glad to see her, he hardly knew what to say.

"Hey," she said, "when do you get off? I need a little masculine advice."

"Really?" He took her hand. "I'm past due for a break."

"Good," she smiled. "Let's go."

"I'm taking a break," Matthew called toward a woman at the front desk as he walked past, holding Melody's hand.

"Looks like the flowers worked," the woman said, and Matthew laughed.

"When do you have to be back?" Melody asked as they stepped outside.

"It's flexible," he said. "I'm supposed to finish the displays, but I can work past closing time as long as I need to."

Melody held up a set of car keys. "Would you test drive it?" she asked, pointing to a little blue sedan.

Matthew laughed again. "It would be a pleasure."

He opened the passenger door for her, then he got in and turned the key. As he drove, she explained, "I lowered my pride and got some help straightening out the mess with the insurance, and a loan to help with a down payment. Between the two, I can get affordable payments."

"Good," he said. "It drives well. I'm no great automobile expert, but if you feel good about it, I think it's a good choice."

He stopped for a few minutes and looked under the hood, then they drove to the dealership. Melody signed the papers and then drove Matthew back toward the sporting goods store. "Thank you," she said. "I appreciate your opinion."

"My pleasure."

"Have you got time for a drink or something?"

"Sure," he said. "Actually, I'm starving."

They stopped for a burger and fries, which Matthew insisted on paying for. As they sat down to eat, Melody asked, "You wouldn't know how some unexplained money got into my wallet, would you?"

Matthew smiled as he said, "I don't know what you're talking about."

"Well, thank you anyway," she said, and he laughed.

"Hey," he said, taking her hand across the table, "it's almost Thanksgiving. I suppose you'll need to be with your family."

"Why?" she asked.

"I was hoping you could come and have dinner with *my* family."

The thought of meeting Matthew Trevor's family provoked a knot in her stomach. "That would be nice, but . . . it's Thanksgiving."

She was relieved when Matthew said nothing more about it. Obviously he assumed that she'd be with her family, and that was fine. This was all moving too fast for her anyway.

* * * * *

While Matthew supervised his little brothers as they set the table for Thanksgiving dinner, he couldn't stop thinking of Melody. Of course, that was typical these days. But he couldn't suppress the urge to call her. He knew as he dialed the number that she wouldn't answer. But she did. "What are you doing there?" he asked.

"Why are you calling me?" she retorted.

"I asked you first."

"I'm enjoying a peaceful holiday," she insisted.

"I thought you were supposed to be with your family."

"I never said that."

Matthew tried to recall their conversation, but he honestly couldn't. "So, you're spending Thanksgiving Day alone? What are you eating? A TV dinner?"

"It's a turkey one, with stuffing."

"Oh, gag!" he said, making a noise to emphasize it. "I'll be over to get you in five minutes."

"Matthew, no," she protested, but he hung up on her.

"Mother," Matthew called, "is it all right if I bring a guest to dinner?"

"Of course, there's plenty."

Caitlin cooed, "Is it Melody?"

"Yes, it's Melody," Matthew answered his sister, "and if you guys don't behave yourselves, you can get somebody else to take you Christmas shopping."

Melody hurried frantically to find something appropriate to wear. While she tried to convince herself that she was angry with Matthew for doing this, a part of her couldn't deny being excited at the prospect of spending this day with him. If only she could survive having to meet his family!

Matthew kissed her forehead when she answered the door, and she marveled freshly at what a gentleman he was. In the car he said, "There's something I need to tell you . . . before we get to my house."

"Okay," she drawled.

"Do you remember that day you were in court . . . and I was there, too?"

"How could I ever forget?" She rolled her eyes and he laughed.

"Well, I told you that I hang around courtrooms a lot . . . which is true. But I didn't mention that . . . well, the one I hang around in the most . . . the one you were in is . . ."

Melody realized he was nervous. For the first time since she'd met him, he actually looked *nervous*.

"Yes?" she urged.

Matthew cleared his throat and got to the point. "My father was the judge who handled your case."

"What?" she shrieked. "Oh, my gosh. Take me home. I'm not going to—"

"Now, listen to me, Melody. What have you got to be afraid of? He's really a very nice man. He probably doesn't even remember it. He goes through dozens of cases every week. And it's not like you were in there for committing a crime, or something."

"Yes, but—"

"I'm not taking you home. You're going to spend Thanksgiving with me whether you like it or not."

"Has anyone ever told you that you're controlling and arrogant, and—"

"No," he said, then he laughed.

Melody wiped her sweating palms over her skirt as Matthew led her up the walk toward the front door. Her nerves subsided some as she surveyed the house where he'd grown up. It was everything she'd expected: big without being huge, with a neatly manicured yard and a two-car garage. A Chevy Suburban sat in the driveway. "I always wanted a Suburban," she said. Matthew chuckled. She still didn't understand why he thought she was so funny.

The moment they walked in, Melody was assaulted by warmth. The atmosphere just rushed around her with the message *home*. She couldn't explain it, but she wasn't certain if she'd ever felt this way before. Two young boys came running and threw themselves into Matthew's arms. He picked them both up as if they weighed nothing and threw them over his shoulders, bouncing them while they giggled and squirmed. A youngish looking middle-aged woman appeared—obviously Matthew's mother—wearing jeans, big slippers, and a red shirt with a snowman appliqued on it. She smiled as she observed her sons, then her eyes took in Melody. Without waiting for any introductions, she stepped forward and held out a hand. "You must be Melody. It's so nice to finally meet you."

Melody gave Matthew a brief skeptical glance as he set his brothers down. She wondered what he'd been telling his family. "It's a pleasure to meet you as well, Mrs. Trevor," she said.

"Oh, call me Janna," she insisted with a little laugh, then she hugged Matthew. "And it's good to see you for more than five minutes a day." She added to Melody, "He sleeps here, but we rarely see him."

"He's a busy man," Melody commented.

Matthew laughed. "I brought Melody over so you could convince her that I'm a nice guy."

"I'll do my best," Janna smiled and walked toward the kitchen. "Make yourself at home, Melody. I'll be in here if you need me."

Matthew took her hand and led her down the stairs to the family room. A teenage girl was preoccupied with a video game, and the loud music emanating from somewhere down the hall was a good clue that the other sister was close by. Long legs clad in blue jeans stuck out from beneath a newspaper. She assumed they were attached to Matthew's father. Her heart quickened with nervousness as Matthew said, "Dad, there's someone I want you to meet."

The newspaper folded down immediately, and Melody caught her breath. Sure enough, she'd seen this man before. And the resemblance to Matthew was startling. Memories rushed over her, and she felt a little queasy.

"Melody, this is my father, Colin Trevor. Dad, this is Melody Morgan."

"Hello, Miss Morgan," he said, coming to his feet with an extended hand.

"Hello," she squeaked, shaking his hand tentatively.

"Have we met?" Colin Trevor asked while she was fighting the urge to hit Matthew.

"I'm afraid we have," she admitted. Then she glared at Matthew. While he was looking sheepish, she turned to his father and said, "Forgive me. Your son didn't bother to mention until a few minutes ago that you're a judge."

"I told you I met her in a courtroom," Matthew said to his father.

"Don't you worry about it, young lady," Colin said. "I left the robe at the office."

Melody relaxed after that. She met Matthew's sisters and his grandmother, who lived nearby. She helped Matthew and his mother in the kitchen, feeling a warmth surround her that she felt certain was something close to heaven.

Matthew's family was kind and accepting of Melody, and it didn't take her long to feel comfortable. Watching his father now, it was almost difficult to comprehend his being a judge. But in spite of the warmth surrounding her, something unexplainably cold and hollow smoldered inside. While she appreciated the opportunity to participate in a *real* Thanksgiving celebration—with a real family—for the first time in her life, she couldn't help feeling bitter, and perhaps just plain heartsick, to think of her own family. She wished they would even make the effort to celebrate holidays; then she realized that even if they did, it would likely be a disaster.

As the turkey was set on the table and the family gathered around it, Melody found it difficult to hold her emotion back. She was reminded of how she'd felt standing in that courtroom, just fighting to keep the tears in check. She found it an ironic twist to hear *Judge Trevor* offer a blessing on the meal. As he expressed gratitude for all his family had been blessed with, the tears rolled silently down Melody's face. She discreetly wiped them away before the prayer was over, but all through the meal she felt her emotion hovering close to the surface.

She finally felt better when the meal was finished. After a trip to the bathroom she helped clear the table and wash the dishes. She was amazed at how the entire family worked together to clean up the mess. In fact, Colin insisted that Janna go relax and let the rest of them do the work. When Janna refused, he picked her up and carried her to the couch, where Melody could hear Janna giggling. Colin returned to the kitchen, muttering lightly to the children, "Your mother's a stubborn woman."

When the work was done, they gathered around the table to play board games until they were all hungry again and pulled everything out to eat leftovers. Melody almost felt as if she was in the middle of a dream. She recalled lying in her bed as a child, trying to imagine what a real family was like. Then one day she'd stopped thinking about it, when such thoughts only depressed her.

When Matthew took her home, Melody thanked him for a beautiful day. He kissed her again on the forehead, and told her he'd call tomorrow. She went inside and cried herself to sleep. She wondered again if being involved with Matthew Trevor was a good idea. The entire experience kept her hovering somewhere between ecstasy and agony. Either way she was plagued with emotions that drained her, and she feared that when all was said and done, the agony would overrule.

Matthew returned home to find that everyone had gone to bed except his mother, who was sitting on the couch reading. "So, what do you think?" he asked, sitting beside her.

"She's a beautiful girl, Matthew."

"Yeah," he chuckled.

"Do you know anything about her family?" Janna asked.

Matthew's brow furrowed. "Not really. She doesn't say much. Why?"

"Well, she's seems fairly confident and well adjusted—at least from what I could tell. But . . . well, maybe I shouldn't say this, but . . . I'd bet money that she's an abuse victim."

Matthew pressed a hand unwillingly over his chest. He'd noticed how guarded Melody was; but in spite of his occasional work at the crisis center, he had totally missed something that was obvious to his mother. Of course, Janna had always been more discerning, and she'd worked with such people for years.

"You really think so?" he asked.

"Yes, I do."

Matthew looked into his mother's eyes, feeling suddenly alarmed. "Are you trying to tell me that I shouldn't get involved with her or—"

"Oh, no, Matthew," she insisted, taking his hand into hers. "She needs someone like you. You, more than most men, have what it takes to deal with whatever she's carrying around."

Matthew drew a deep breath, finding some peace in his mother's words without fully understanding why.

"By the way you were looking at her all day," his mother said, "I assume your feelings are . . ." She left the statement open for him to finish.

"Incredible," he said. "Overwhelming. Undeniable. Like nothing I've ever felt in my life."

Janna smiled and squeezed his hand.

Matthew didn't see Melody again until Sunday, since he had to work long hours over the weekend. They went to church together—in her ward, since she was filling in for an absent Primary teacher. He sat in the classroom with her while she taught seven nine-year-olds. Occasionally he intervened to help keep the children quiet, and rather enjoyed himself. Observing Melody this way, it was easy to see her potential. She'd said she wanted a degree in elementary education. Matthew could see that she was gifted at teaching young children by the way she interacted with them. But his mind was more drawn to the idea that she would make an incredible mother.

After church, they went back to Melody's apartment and cooked spaghetti together. Matthew enjoyed the day and found it only increased his desire to be with her every possible minute. They began to see each other regularly; little by little she warmed up to him, and Matthew's longing to be with her only deepened. In spite of her adamant avoidance of any activity related to Christmas, it became increasingly evident that Melody's testimony was strong in the gospel. She talked of her hopes for the future in a way that made Matthew tingle at the thought of sharing that future with her. But no matter how he tried, he couldn't get her to talk about the past. Any questions about her family and upbringing were cleverly evaded.

One evening over a chili dog and a malt, Matthew declared, "Tomorrow I'd like to take you to this nativity concert thing on the Tabernacle lawn."

Melody wrinkled her nose, saying, "Why don't you go ring your own jingle bells?"

Matthew laughed and took her hand. "Listen, Miss Scrooge, I've humored your evasion of Christmas long enough. I *love* Christmas and everything to do with it. If you're not going to put up with it, you'll have to find another boyfriend."

"Boyfriend?" she retorted. "What makes you think you're my *boyfriend?*"

"Is there some other guy you're seeing every day, and holding his hand everywhere you go?"

"No."

"Well, there you have it. And you must like a guy quite a bit to have Thanksgiving dinner with his family."

"You practically forced me," she clarified.

"Well, you've refused to go back since. Were they that deplorable?"

Melody didn't like the way he'd just described *her* family. "No, they were perfectly charming."

"So it's *me* that's deplorable," he stated.

"What are you talking about?"

"I want to know why you won't go to the concert with me."

"I've told you. I *hate* Christmas."

"And I *love* Christmas."

"Well, then maybe you should look for somebody else to hold hands with."

"I don't want to hold anybody else's hand, Melody Noel Morgan."

"How did you know my middle name?"

"I sneaked a peek at your driver's license," he smirked.

"Oh, is that when you sneaked money into my wallet?"

"Me?" His eyes widened with exaggerated shock. "You know, for a Christmas baby, you're sure a Scrooge."

45

"Yes, I am. What are you going to do about it?"

"I'm going to take you to the nativity concert tomorrow. We're going to have to finish Christmas shopping. And there are some Christmas movies that you absolutely have to watch with me. It's a tradition. And then, this coming Saturday we're going to make Christmas goodies at my house—and decorate the tree, and stuff like that."

Melody wanted to ask what exactly a *Christmas goody* was, but she didn't want to draw attention to her ignorance. Instead she snarled lightly, "And what if I don't?"

"I'll arrange for the ghost of Christmas present to visit you every night when the bell tolls one, and . . ." He stopped when her expression clearly told him she had no idea what he was talking about. "Surely you know the story of Ebenezer Scrooge."

"Not really. I just know he has a reputation."

"A reputation that you exemplify very well, my dear. I'm going to teach you to like Christmas yet."

"Yeah, whether I want to or not."

"Exactly," he said and couldn't help laughing.

"What's so funny?" she demanded.

"You are. I've never seen anybody look so completely adorable when they're angry." She scowled at him and he added, "I'll pick you up tomorrow at six-thirty. Dress warm."

When Matthew went to Melody's apartment to get her, he almost expected her not to be there, or perhaps refuse to go. But she met him at the door, bundled up for the cold weather. "I hate Christmas," she said lightly, but her eyes were serious.

"I know," he said, keeping it light himself as they walked to the car. "That's why I'm taking you to this thing. I'm trying to torture you as much as possible until the dreaded day arrives. And with any luck, you'll learn something."

"Oh, and just what do you expect me to learn?"

"When you learn it, you'll know."

The night was cold and clear as they walked around the Tabernacle to where bleachers were set up on the lawn. Matthew put one blanket over their laps and another around their shoulders, with his arm around Melody. She didn't think too much about the presentation, but she enjoyed the warmth of Matthew's nearness and the way it seemed to symbolize her feelings at the moment. As long as she was with Matthew Trevor, she felt somehow safe from the cold, cruel world.

When the concert was over, they took the blankets back to the car, then they walked across Center Street to the Hallmark store. "Oh, I'm not going in there," she protested.

"And why not?" Matthew argued.

"I hate that store, *especially* at Christmastime."

"It's positively the most cheerful little store in town."

"I know," she said, "and I'm not in the mood to be cheerful."

"Oh, come on, Scrooge," he countered. "Just for a few minutes."

Melody scowled at Matthew but followed him inside. She tried to keep herself from feeling the inevitable ache. It erupted each time she was reminded that Christmas meant nothing to her. And she knew it should mean *something*. It obviously meant something to Matthew. In fact, it meant something to everyone she'd ever known—except her own family. A part of her wanted to change the way she felt, but she didn't know how.

While Matthew perused Christmas cards, occasionally showing her one that was especially funny or sweet, Melody stood with her hands in her coat pockets, trying to keep herself somehow detached from the atmosphere. She closed her eyes, but she could still hear Christmas music floating around her. She briefly put her gloved hands over her ears, but the place even *smelled* like Christmas.

When Matthew turned his attention to the dozens of collectible Christmas ornaments lining one wall, she was tempted to just walk outside and wait for him. But he held her hand tightly, as if he knew exactly what she was thinking. He pointed to some mechanical ornaments, saying, "Now you have to admit these are cute."

"Yes, they're cute," she said curtly.

Distracting herself from Christmas, Melody became caught up in observing Matthew. He examined the contents of the little store with the innocence of a child. She longed to have that kind of innocence. Although she knew from experience that he had a great deal of maturity and wisdom, she felt certain he was clueless about what the world was really like.

Matthew distracted Melody from her thoughts as he pointed to a round ornament depicting a couple in a sleigh. She looked closer to see that it said *Our First Christmas Together,* along with the date. "You should buy me one of these," he said with a smirk.

"At this rate, it will be our *last* Christmas together," she said. "If we even make it until then."

"You just wait and see," he said, leading her toward the door.

"No, *you* just wait and see."

They walked the long way around the block to where the car was parked, ambling slowly past the trees lining the street, filled with thousands of twinkling Christmas lights. They were almost to the car when Matthew stopped walking and turned her to face him. She held her breath as it became evident that he intended to kiss her. She almost dreaded it, knowing that every relationship from her past had somehow lost its magic once they'd kissed. She had only known kisses that were lusty and sordid. And past that point, every man she'd ever known had seemed to want only one thing, and she'd had to fight terribly hard to keep her virtue intact. But something surprising happened when Matthew Trevor pressed his lips to hers. The gentlemanly manner he'd always shown toward her only deepened. She'd never considered the possibility that a kiss could be spiritual, but this one was. Everything about it was meek and tentative, yet she could almost feel the promise hovering beneath it. *Like the kiss of an angel,* she thought, and tears crept into her eyes.

Matthew pulled back to look at her and she willed the emotion back, grateful that it was too dark for him to see her expression clearly.

"Melody," he whispered, the tone of his voice adding to the hypnotic feel of the moment, "I'm falling in love with you." Her eyes widened and he laughed softly. "Falling?" He laughed again. "Allow me to correct myself. I *fell*. I fell hard and fast the minute I saw you walk out of that courtroom." His expression sobered. His voice deepened. "I love you, Melody."

Melody didn't even realize there were tears on her face until Matthew wiped them away. "Is something wrong?" he asked.

"Nobody's ever told me that before and meant it."

Matthew's brow furrowed. "Nobody?"

She shook her head. Matthew pulled her close to him, wishing he could somehow magically erase the hurt in her life, whatever it might be.

"Well, I *mean* it, Melody. I love you. I cannot even imagine life without you. You're everything I've ever wanted."

Melody absorbed the implication and stepped back abruptly, startling him. "You don't have any idea what you're talking about. You know practically nothing about me. How could you possibly know if I'm everything you want?"

"I just *know.*"

"You're thinking with your heart," she insisted.

"And what's wrong with that?"

"I believe that heart and head have to agree," she stated.

"I can go along with that."

"And you don't have enough information to know whether or not your heart is out in left field."

"Okay, so give me some information, Melody. Talk to me."

Melody turned away from him, more afraid than she dared admit. Matthew put his hands on her shoulders, whispering behind her ear, as if he'd read her thoughts, "What are you afraid of, Melody?"

Melody tried to answer that in her own mind. Was she afraid of losing him if he knew the truth? Or losing him if she kept avoiding the truth? Either way, there was only one option: she had to be honest. But she wasn't certain if either one of them was ready for it.

Chapter Five

"It's too cold out here to talk," Melody said, attempting to evade the conversation. But Matthew walked her back to the car and turned it on to let the heater run.

"Okay," he said, turning to face her. "It'll be getting warm in here pretty quick. We can talk now."

Several minutes elapsed in miserable silence. While Melody tried to find a suitable place to begin telling him the truth about her life, she sensed his growing frustration.

Matthew finally said, "What's the deal, Melody? What do I have to do to make you trust me?"

"What makes you think I don't trust you?"

"You have told me absolutely nothing about yourself or your family. You tell me you have family here in town, but I've yet to meet one of them. I get the feeling that you like me, but at the same time, you don't want to have anything to do with me. I love you, Melody. I think I loved you the minute I saw you. But I can't take living on a one-way street."

"Okay, fine," she snarled. "I guess a person can only hide from the truth for so long." She took a deep breath, certain that once she got all of this out, she would never see him again. "I haven't taken you to meet my family because I am embarrassed, Matthew. If you took one look at what I came from, you would be horrified."

Matthew sighed. "I'm listening," he said in a soft voice.

"I don't know where to begin, Matthew."

"Okay, how about if I ask you a simple question."

"One question?"

"If you give me a complete, honest answer, I'll only ask one question—for now."

"I've never been dishonest with you."

"I know. It's the *complete* you seem to have trouble with."

She scowled at him then glanced away. "Okay, one question."

"Why do you hate Christmas?" She looked alarmed and he clarified. "I've seen evidence that you live your religion, Melody; a religion based solely on Christ. This is the time of year we celebrate his life and all he did for us. Why is that so difficult for you?"

"You don't have to celebrate Christmas to be a Christian," she countered.

"And you don't have to be a Christian to celebrate Christmas. But I have heard our prophet say that life is meant to be enjoyed, not just endured. Christmas is an opportunity to enjoy and share the good things provided for us in this beautiful world."

Melody became so caught up in what he was saying that she almost forgot for a moment how much she hated Christmas.

"You know what I find interesting?" he went on. "I once added it up on a calendar. The Christmas season is just about 5.2 weeks out of the year. Ten percent. Now, if you understand the concept of tithing, isn't it interesting that we spend ten percent of our lives celebrating the greatest event in history?"

When he was obviously finished and waiting for a response, Melody felt her nerves rise again. "You'll make a great lawyer," she insisted. "I feel like I've been convicted."

Matthew sighed and willed himself not to get frustrated. The last thing he wanted was for her to try and walk home again.

Melody looked at her hands, folded in her lap. "I'm sorry." She sighed and forced herself to explain. "It's not so much the meaning of Christmas as the celebrating itself, I suppose."

When she didn't go on, Matthew said, "I'm listening."

"We never had Christmas in my home, Matthew. It's as simple as that."

"What? Because there was no money? Was it—"

"Money was scarce; there's no question about that. But we just . . . didn't have Christmas. I remember hearing stories of poor families celebrating with practically nothing; stories that always emphasized the love and giving in a family, in spite of not having material things. But that wasn't the case in my home. There was never a tree; not even a pine bough. We had no Christmas decorations. There were no gifts. No music. Not even a special meal. There wasn't even an acknowledgment that December twenty-fifth was different from any other day. While the kids on the street were comparing what Santa had brought them, I was usually mopping the floor or something." Matthew watched her eyes become hollow and distant as she spoke. His palms began to sweat and his mouth went dry as he attempted to comprehend the reality of what she was saying.

"One year my mother pulled a little sack out of the closet and handed it to me. She just said, 'Here's a little

Christmas present for you.' It wasn't wrapped. There was no pomp or ceremony. *Nothing.*"

Matthew attempted to come up with something to say that might console her somehow. But it only took a moment to know that *nothing* he could say would erase the heartache of her past.

Melody caught her breath as Matthew pulled her into his arms without warning, holding her as if he might die without her. She wasn't certain of his motives, but the giving in his embrace warmed her through. She drew back to look into his eyes, surprised by the genuine emotion she saw there. Without a word spoken, she knew that he truly cared. Hesitant to let him go, she laid her head on his shoulder and sighed. It was easy now to share her thoughts.

"I often used to fantasize about what it might be like to wake up Christmas morning and find stockings filled by the stove, and a Christmas tree in the house, all decorated and lit up, with a big package beneath it, wrapped in shiny red paper, just for me."

When she said nothing more, Matthew asked in a shaky voice, "What did you want to have in it, Melody?"

She laughed softly; it was a laugh with no sign of pleasure or humor. "I always wanted my very own, brand-new coat. Every coat I ever owned was handed down or purchased used. Most of my coats had belonged to my older brothers. It wasn't bad enough that I had to wear a used coat, it had to be a *boy's* coat. I had an older sister, but she was such a tomboy that she preferred to wear boys' clothes anyway."

Matthew tightened his arm around her while a tangible ache rose inside of him.

"I saved money to buy my own coat," she went on. "I'd go door to door, begging for work. I think some of the people in our neighborhood actually felt sorry for me. I'd do anything that anybody would pay me for. But every time I got almost enough, something would happen. More than once my brother stole it from me. Another time my father took it and bought me shoes instead; the ugliest shoes I'd ever seen. Then one day I just gave up. I resigned myself to wearing old coats, and I've had to struggle a great deal to convince myself that if you work hard for something you might actually get it. I have everything I need and much to be grateful for. I've managed to make a life for myself. I've come a long way, but . . ." Her voice faded with a sigh.

There was so much Matthew wanted to say, but he settled for simply asking, "Did you *ever* get a new coat?"

"Are you kidding? The older I got, the more I had to struggle just to survive. I don't know if I've ever had a new *anything.*"

"Then you have something to look forward to," he said.

"What's that supposed to mean?" she asked, raising her head to look at him.

Matthew smiled. "The future is as bright as you make it, Melody. And with any luck, you'll let me be a part of it."

"We're completely incompatible," she insisted, putting distance between them.

"Why? Because I love Christmas and you hate it?"

"That's one reason."

"Well, you know what, Melody Noel? You've got a thing or two to learn about Christmas. But I think you're actually doing pretty good with life in general. And how can you hate something you don't even know? It's not Christmas you hate, Melody. It's being on the outside of something you've never experienced. It's the absence of Christmas in your life that's hard for you."

"And what are you going to do about it?"

"I intend to show you what Christmas is all about. Whether or not you and I ever get past New Year's Day, I'm going to give you a Christmas you'll never forget."

"Now listen to me, Matthew. The last thing I want is for you to feel sorry for me and go out and spend money to—"

He pressed his fingers over her lips. "It has nothing to do with money, Melody. And I'm going to prove it to you."

"Oh, and how are you going to do that?"

"You just wait and see."

Melody couldn't help being intrigued by Matthew's promise. But apprehension set in when he insisted that she spend Saturday with his family.

"It's our annual get-ready-for-Christmas day," he declared. "It's almost as fun as Christmas Day itself."

"Oh, that sounds just great," she said with sarcasm. "But I don't *do* Christmas."

"Hey, you'll love it."

"Don't tell me what I'll love, Matthew Trevor. If I'm in the mood to be depressed, I can be depressed. If I want to hate Christmas, nobody can stop me."

She had intended to be serious, but it came out sounding so ridiculous that she couldn't hold back a little chuckle. Matthew laughed and kissed her quickly. "I'll have you ringing jingle bells yet," he smirked, and she almost believed him.

Melody didn't sleep well Friday night. Her memories merged with her concerns for the future until she had difficulty even thinking straight. Logically, she had no trouble accepting that distancing herself from her family had been the right thing. But her heart continued to ache for them. A part of her almost felt guilty for seeking out a good life, knowing they were all struggling so much. She reminded herself that they had all made their own choices, just as she had. And she knew it was not in her power to take away their agency. But still, her heart ached. By morning she began to wonder if part of the reason she found it so difficult to enjoy Christmas was simply the guilt created by knowing that those who were her own flesh and blood would have no Christmas at all.

In spite of her difficult night, Melody was up and ready to go when Matthew came to get her at nine. Just seeing him made everything seem a little better. She loved the way he held her hand as they drove across town to his home. She didn't feel the least bit apprehensive until they arrived. Then, as she walked through the front door, the sounds and smells of Christmas assaulted her. The air was thick with a combination of pine, spices, and a warm oven. Christmas music wafted from a distant stereo. She hesitated in the doorway, trying to will the habitual tension away.

"Come on," Matthew urged, taking both her hands into his. He kicked the door closed and walked backward into the house, pulling her along. With that grin on his face, she might think he was leading her into heaven itself. He squeezed her hands tightly and warmth tingled over her. The gesture felt familiar somehow, though she didn't understand why.

They greeted his parents, who were both in the kitchen, mixing a huge bowl of batter. Colin stirred while Janna added ingredients. Melody was about to ask what it was, at the risk of appearing ignorant, when Janna said, "As soon as the fruitcakes are done, we'll start rolling out cookies."

They found Jake and Dustin in the front room, taping red and green paper into chains. Matthew stopped to show them how to use little pieces of tape instead of stringing it all over the place, then he escorted Melody to the Christmas tree.

"This is the angel tree," he announced, and Melody gasped as she absorbed it. The tree was artificial, but you could hardly see it for the ribbons and decorations hanging there. Everything was gold and white, and every ornament was some kind of angel.

"My parents bought this at the Festival of Trees a few years ago," he explained. "It was something my father always wanted to do. The money goes to the children's hospital. We don't even undecorate it. We just cover the whole thing with plastic and put it in the storage room."

Melody became so fascinated with the tree that she was startled when Matthew asked, "Do you know why they depict angels with wings?"

She answered while touching a tiny ceramic angel hanging from gold thread. "It symbolizes their being heavenly messengers."

"Very good," he drawled. "Especially for someone who doesn't like Christmas."

"Oh, angels aren't limited to Christmas," she said with a little smile that aroused Matthew's curiosity. He was wondering how to ask where her thoughts were when she turned to him, saying, "But I always imagined them wearing armor."

He was even more curious now, but Caitlin hollered his name.

"What?" he called back.

She appeared in the front room. "Dad said to tell you to bring the tree in."

"Okay, I'm coming." At Melody's inquisitive gaze he added, "The *real* Christmas tree goes in the family room."

Melody followed Matthew outside and watched as he trimmed the trunk of an evergreen tree with a hatchet to make it fit into the tree stand. She'd always wondered how people made those things stand up in their houses.

When the tree was securely in the stand, he pulled on a pair of leather gloves, picked up the whole thing, and headed toward the house. Melody held the door open for him, and the family gathered to follow the tree to its resting place in the family room. Everyone seemed excited, especially the young boys. And Melody couldn't help but feel their anticipation. She stood back and mostly observed as Caitlin and Mallory maneuvered the lights into the prickly branches. They complained of getting pricked by pine needles and finding pine gum on their fingers. But they kept laughing as they worked together to string the lights around and around the circumference of the tree. Jake and Dustin pulled out every ornament while Matthew tried to keep them in some kind of order. Melody noticed Colin and Janna cuddled up on the couch watching, as if they were as young and in love as she and Matthew.

Melody began to think they'd never get those lights put on the tree. But Caitlin finally declared it was done, and Mallory plugged them in. Everyone gasped as the tree lit up, then they began adding garland and tinsel. Melody enjoyed her observations of Matthew with his siblings, trying not to feel the empty ache each time she tried to compare this experience to her own family life. She was surprised when he held a shiny red and gold ornament in front of her face, saying, "You need to put this one on."

"Why me?" she asked.

"Read it."

Melody squinted to read the faded script that encircled the little ball. *Christmas is a place in your heart.*

Melody fought back a rush of emotion. Matthew motioned elaborately toward the tree. She took a deep breath and hung it carefully on a branch.

Matthew watched her closely and knew beyond any doubt that she had never done that before in her life. He wondered how a person could exist for twenty years in the United States of America and never hang a Christmas ornament. And she wasn't even Jewish.

"I love you, Melody Noel," he whispered. She only smiled and asked if she could do another one. Matthew laughed and handed her one after another. When the ornaments were on, Janna passed out handfuls of shiny plastic icicles. Matthew almost felt moved to tears as he watched Melody's eyes light up like a child's each time she strung a silver icicle over a branch of the tree.

When the tree was finished and the fruitcakes were cooling, the family gathered in the kitchen to roll out Christmas cookies. Again Melody's countenance glowed with childlike innocence as she watched Janna roll out the buttery dough and cut it into little trees and bells and stars.

"Have you ever done this before?" Matthew whispered, and she shook her head slightly. Melody was almost afraid to speak for fear of having her emotion erupt. For years she had avoided anything related to Christmas, not wanting to feel the reality of what she'd missed. That empty ache had always spurred emotion, and she had gone to great lengths to avoid feeling it. Today her emotion hovered uncomfortably near the surface, but rather than fearing it, she almost encouraged it. Today's ache was a different kind; rather than brooding over what she had missed, she wanted to absorb it all and savor it forever. She wanted to touch and taste and smell and hear and see *everything* about Christmas. While a part of her couldn't help thinking of the tragedy of her childhood, something bigger was filling her with gratitude for what she was now experiencing. She watched Matthew interacting with his family and competently taking his turn at rolling the cookie dough. She wondered if it might actually be possible to spend the rest of her life with him—and eternity as well. The thought spurred more emotion, and she had to swallow hard to keep from sobbing.

When the cookies were baked and cooled, and the family had pitched in to clean up the mess, they gathered around the table to frost and decorate. Melody watched the others for a few minutes before Matthew set some cookies in front of her and put a knife in her hand. When she looked apprehensive, Matthew wrapped his hand around hers, taking her through the motions of putting fluffy white frosting on a star-shaped cookie. "See how easy that is," he said with a little smirk. Then he sprinkled red and green sugar on it.

Feeling a need to lighten her mood, Melody held the cookie up close to his mouth. As he took a bite she shoved it in his face, leaving frosting all over his mouth and nose. It was difficult to tell who laughed hardest: The children. His parents. Or Melody as she held her side, watching Matthew glare at her—even though he was laughing himself. Then, without warning, he pulled her face into his hands and kissed her with a loud smooch, leaving an equal amount of frosting on *her* face, while his family cheered and applauded. Matthew laughed as she wiped it off with her finger and tasted it. "Ooh, it's good," she said.

Janna handed them each a wet washcloth to clean their faces, saying, "It reminds me of the way I fed your father wedding cake."

"Oh, I remember," Matthew chuckled.

Melody was going to ask how Matthew might remember his parents' wedding, but she became distracted by the silent message in his eyes. The reference to weddings was both frightening and exciting.

When the antics died down, Melody carefully covered a tree-shaped cookie with green frosting. Then she squiggled colored lines on it from a decorator tube, and put little candy silver balls and colored sprinkles over it. Feeling rather proud of herself, she glanced up at Matthew to find him watching her. Without a word spoken, she somehow knew that he understood what she was feeling. The feeling in his expression was so evident that her own emotion erupted, and the tears fell before she even had a chance to think about holding them back. Just when she thought she could discreetly dry her tears and get out of the room, a tear rolled down Matthew's cheek. Oblivious to his family's presence, he pulled her into his arms and pressed his lips into her hair while she cried helplessly.

"Why is Melody crying, Mom?" Dustin asked with perfect five-year-old innocence.

"I don't know, Dustin," Janna answered quietly.

"Matthew," Dustin asked, "why is Melody crying?"

Matthew continued to hold her as he answered, "Melody has never frosted Christmas cookies, Dusty. Or decorated a tree. I think she's sad because she never got to do those things when she was a little girl."

"Never?" Jake asked incredulously.

"I don't know." Matthew nudged Melody and repeated, "Never?"

She shook her head and continued to cry. "It's okay," he whispered, but she stood up and hurried into the bathroom.

Matthew absorbed the stunned expressions of his family members. His mother had tears in her eyes.

"Why?" Mallory asked. "Were they just poor or—"

"Yeah," Matthew said, "I think they were. But I think the problem was more that they were poor in spirit as well."

"What does that mean?" Jake asked.

"I'll explain it to you later," Janna said, hearing the bathroom door open. She added in a whisper, "Just keep doing what you were doing."

They all took the hint and behaved as if nothing was wrong when Melody returned—except Dustin. As Melody sat down and Matthew took her hand, the child asked, "Melody, were you crying because you never got to decorate a cookie when you were little?"

As Matthew squeezed her hand, Melody answered softly, "That's part of it, Dustin. But I think it was more that I'm very happy to be able to do it now." She smiled up at Matthew and wondered if life could be better than this.

Chapter Six

Melody didn't see Matthew much the next several days. Their work schedules and his studies made it practically impossible. But he called her every day, and Melody found that every little bit of evidence that he was in her life somehow made the future brighter.

On Thursday evening he stopped by the video store, asking in a serious voice, "Do you know where I could rent a movie?" He laughed at the mild disgust in her expression. Then he informed her that they were going to watch their first movie of the *Annual Matthew Trevor Christmas Film Festival*. The following evening he came by her apartment with a video tape, a pizza, and microwave popcorn. Before they started the movie he presented her with a copy of the book *A Christmas Carol*.

"It's not very long," he said. "I want you to read it before we see the movie."

"What? Tonight?"

"No," he laughed. "We're saving *Scrooge* for last. You've got a while yet."

Melody looked at him dubiously. She thanked him for the book, but she didn't make any promises. Together they watched the colorized version of the old *Miracle on 34th Street*. Melody said little, but she looked bored through most of it.

"Well?" he asked when it was over and she turned off the TV.

"Well what? It was okay. Are you trying to tell me that you believe Santa Claus really exists?"

Matthew laughed. "My mother always said, 'If you don't believe, you won't receive.'" He laughed again. "So, I'll tell you what I believe."

"I suspected you would."

"Santa Claus is a personification of the spirit of Christmas; a giver of gifts who has chosen Christ's birthday as the day when he spins his magic. And he has a lot in common with the ghost of Christmas present."

"Excuse me?"

"That's another movie. We're saving that one for last . . . Mademoiselle Scrooge."

Melody hit him with a throw pillow. He laughed and pushed her arms behind her back. She laughed with him until he kissed her and looked into her eyes. "I love you, Melody," he said.

She made a noise of disbelief and squirmed away. "You've barely known me a few weeks."

"Maybe. Maybe not."

"What's that supposed to mean?"

"Maybe we knew each other in the preexistence. Maybe you promised yourself to me and begged me to find you and rescue you from the anti-Christmas syndrome."

Melody laughed and couldn't resist the urge to kiss him back. While she felt hesitant to admit it aloud, she knew she was hopelessly in love. A month ago she'd never heard the name Matthew Trevor. And now the thought of not having him in her future was terrifying.

The following day was Saturday, so they had a movie marathon, beginning with *How the Grinch Stole Christmas.* "That's it!" he said, pausing the video somewhere in the middle. "You're not a Scrooge, you're a Grinch!"

"Oh, thank you very much, Matthew," she said with sarcasm.

He teased her by mimicking the narrator. "It could be her shoes were a little too tight, or maybe her head wasn't screwed on just right."

Melody retorted too seriously, "Or maybe her heart was two sizes too small."

Matthew took her chin into his hand and looked into her eyes. "There's nothing wrong with your heart, or your head, Melody Morgan. And I'm going to prove it."

She grabbed the remote control from him. "Just watch the show."

When it was over, Matthew commented while changing video tapes, "You know, even the Grinch learned to love Christmas in the end. And Scrooge did, too."

"Bah, humbug!" she muttered, and he laughed.

Their little film festival ended that evening with *It's a Wonderful Life.* Matthew felt some hope when Melody cried at the end. He turned off the TV and she kept crying.

"Well?" he asked, as he did after every movie.

"It's pathetically sappy, and . . ."

"And?"

"It was so sweet. Maybe it's because I have a certain fondness for angels."

"Really?" he asked, intrigued.

"I'll tell you some other time," she insisted.

"You don't believe in Santa Claus, but you believe in angels."

With serious eyes she said, "Yes, Matthew, I believe in angels."

His curiosity was evident, but she changed the subject. It was difficult to say good night when he finally left, but he invited her to have dinner with his family the next day. Rather than feeling apprehensive, she was actually looking forward to it. But as they walked into the house after church, Melody felt that familiar knot inside at the evidence of Christmas that assaulted her. She wondered, as she often had, why she found it so difficult to enjoy the holiday. She considered herself a logical person, and she had been able to overcome many of the struggles associated with her upbringing. So why was Christmas still such a sore point? She had enjoyed her time in Matthew's home, and relished the opportunity to be a part of the Christmas preparations. She believed that she'd taken steps toward healing. But even now, she had to consciously will away an ache that began to smolder inside her at the evidence of Christmas surrounding her. Concentrating instead on the experience of being with Matthew and his family, she tried to relax and enjoy herself.

As Matthew discreetly watched Melody across the dinner table, he felt an indescribable warmth. She interacted with his family as if she belonged there. He was beginning to believe what he had wanted to believe from the start. He felt relatively confident that she was the woman for him. Eternity almost seemed comprehensible when he looked into Melody Morgan's eyes.

When dinner was over, Melody insisted on helping with the dishes. Matthew helped clear the table, watching the way she bustled around the kitchen. She obviously knew how to work and wasn't afraid to do it—even in somebody else's home. He heard her laugh at something his mother said, and a warm tingle skittered down his spine.

When Jake chased Dustin into the kitchen, Janna said to Matthew, "Will you please entertain the little beasts while we finish up here?"

Matthew opened his mouth to protest, wanting to be near Melody. But his mother gave him a subtle look that seemed to imply she wanted time for girl talk.

"Okay, I can take a hint," he said, sauntering dramatically out of the kitchen as if he felt dejected. "Just don't say anything bad about me."

Nearly an hour later, Melody found Matthew sorting through sports cards with his little brothers.

"That must have been one hefty batch of dishes," Matthew said.

"It sure was," she said lightly, then added in a quiet voice, "You were right. Your mother's an incredible woman."

"She's you in twenty years," Matthew said again.

"I'm not so sure," Melody insisted, certain that Janna Trevor had always been strong and confident. She couldn't imagine her any other way.

Matthew's mind wandered to his earlier thoughts. He had the urge to just propose here and now, but he felt like it might be wise to give their relationship a little more time. Instead, he ventured a step in the right direction.

"When are you going to take me to meet *your* family?"

Melody felt her expression fall with her mood. "Trust me, Matthew. It's just not a good idea."

"Why not? Are you ashamed of me?"

Melody turned to study his expression. He was *serious*. A one-syllable laugh erupted out of her mouth as she perceived the irony of his statement.

Matthew felt confused at her response. Attempting to clarify, he asked, "Is there some reason you don't want your parents to meet me? Am I—"

"Listen, Matthew," she began. Then, remembering that they weren't alone, she took his hand and stood up. "Is there someplace private where we can talk?"

Matthew led her to a bedroom that was obviously his and closed the door. "Okay, talk," he said, sitting on the floor.

Melody sat on the chair near the desk and took a deep breath. Trying to come up with an appropriate explanation, she admitted, "I really hate this."

"Well, so do I," he said. "I'm beginning to feel like there's something wrong with me, and you just don't—"

"Well, let me start by saying that you are *way* off base."

"Then let me meet your parents, Melody."

"Why? Why is it so important?"

"They're your parents! Shouldn't they know there's a man in your life who's madly in love with you and—"

"They don't care, Matthew, I can assure you."

Matthew couldn't even respond to that. He couldn't question what she was saying; he had no reason to think she would tell him anything but the truth. But he couldn't even comprehend somebody *not caring* about this woman he loved.

Melody studied Matthew's determined, confused expression and knew she couldn't avoid this any longer. She sighed and pressed a hand through the full length of her dark hair. "Okay, fine. Let me tell you about my family."

"I wish you would."

"My father is dead, Matthew."

Matthew's eyes widened. That statement alone made him realize how ignorant she had kept him. Before he could comment, she continued.

"He was a severe alcoholic. He literally drank himself to the grave. The details are not worth repeating. My mother doesn't drink. But she devotes her entire existence to doing everything in her power to keep her children from complaining. She has two grown sons—my older brothers—who sit at her house watching television, smoking and drinking beer, and eating away at her Social Security. I have an older sister who has two illegitimate children. The state finally took them away from her due to neglect. It didn't take much effort to get her to sign them away. They've now been adopted by a wonderful couple, I'm happy to say. And she's moved to Mexico since her live-in boyfriend was an illegal alien and got deported. My younger sister steals money from me to buy beer and cigarettes—and I suspect illegal substances—for her boyfriend, who I have yet to see sober. Right now she is pregnant and can't understand why I'm not happy about it. I mean, the father has no intention of marrying her. I'm relatively certain he's a gang member, and his hobbies include collecting tattoos and piercing various parts of his body.

"My little sister is really good at shoplifting as well. I got caught with her more than once. One time she sneaked the stuff into my bag, and I actually went to jail. I have a police record, Matthew. And your father is a judge. That puts you and me on opposite sides of the tracks. Are you getting the picture here?"

Matthew's expression was completely unreadable as she finished. When he said nothing for more than a minute, she finally asked, "Well, don't you have anything to say?"

"Yeah, I can beat that."

"What do you mean *you can beat that?*"

"I can beat it. I've got a few skeletons in my closet."

"Okay, but I don't think you can beat it."

"Okay, maybe I can't *beat* it. I guess such things are relative. But I certainly don't have a spotless past."

"So, what did you do? Steal a candy bar when you were seven? Sneak past a *No Trespassing* sign?"

"No, I did that when I was nine."

Melody sighed with disgust. Matthew leaned forward, and the expression in his eyes caught her attention. "Melody," he took her hand, "I was born illegitimate, for one thing."

Melody laughed, certain he had to be joking. When his expression remained sober, she stopped abruptly. "You're serious."

"Yes, I'm serious. I was born Matthew Hayne. My mother was not married."

Melody tried to imagine what this meant about Janna Trevor. Deciding it was a joke, she insisted, "But . . . you look so much like . . . your father. If he's . . ."

"Oh, he's my biological father. But he was not my mother's first husband. That's why there are so many years between me and Caitlin."

Melody felt a softening inside her for reasons she couldn't explain as Matthew told her the story in a soft voice. "You see, my parents were high school sweethearts. The spring before my mother graduated, her mother died. And that same night, they had a passionate escapade. They went straight to talk to the bishop, and three months later my mother left to live with an aunt in Arizona. She lied to my father. She wanted him to go on a mission and become a lawyer. And he did, with no idea that I existed. I was nearly seven before my father knew he had a son. And there are other aspects to that story that you should hear from my mother."

"Why?" she asked.

"Because it's *her* story." When Melody said nothing, Matthew touched her face. "Here's a lesson in judgment, Melody. I don't claim to have lived through what you have, and I'm grateful to have such a good family. But there are things about us that you might be surprised at. Things are not necessarily what they appear, and good things come out of bad situations and bad places. You are a shining example of that."

"Example?" she squeaked. "Haven't you been listening to me? I come from at least three generations of codependent, alcoholic losers."

"I heard you, Melody. But maybe you've missed something. It's easy for people who grow up loved and happy to become successful; to live their religion. But to rise above those kinds of circumstances to do the same is more admirable than I could find words to describe. I mean, look at you. You're twenty years old. You've got a good job, and you're completely supporting yourself. I'm still living with my parents, for crying out loud. I'm paying my own tuition and expenses, but I'm not sure I'd be able to do it if I had to live on my own."

Melody was speechless. In all her years of struggling to be a good girl in spite of her circumstances, she'd never once considered such a concept. While she was trying to come up with a response, he asked, "How did you do it, Melody? What makes you different from the rest of them?"

"I don't know. I just . . . never felt comfortable with that lifestyle. I always believed there was something better."

"That's because you're one of those strong spirits who instinctively knows right from wrong in spite of whatever life might give you." He touched her face with such obvious adoration that she felt certain he'd missed something somewhere. "You're like a flower blooming in a mud puddle."

Melody glanced down, suddenly seized by an unexplainable emotion. Matthew lifted her chin to make her face him. "Tell me about it, Melody. Tell me how a flower blooms in a mud puddle."

"I don't know," she chuckled uncomfortably, still trying to comprehend his attitude. "I just . . . well, there was this widow who lived down the street. Sister Thompson. She was in her early seventies when I first met her, I believe, but always very healthy and independent for her age. Just after I turned seven she was made the Primary secretary. She was also my mother's visiting teacher. One day she just knocked at the door and asked my mother to go to church with her. My mother was full of excuses. Of course, Dad wouldn't let her go. But Sister Thompson insisted on taking us kids to Primary. I'll never forget how she marched up to my father and stared him down. I always wished my mother could have stood up to him that way. She just told him she was going to take the children to church with her, and wondered if he had a problem with that. He told her it was fine, as long as they didn't come home trying to preach to him."

Melody's eyes grew distant as the memories hovered closer. "The others went for a few weeks, but one at a time they lost interest. When my little sister got old enough to go, she really seemed to like it. For a long time I believed she would come through. But something went wrong somewhere, and eventually she stopped going like the others. But I loved it. When I was in that church building, I felt like a real person. I thrived on the stories and the songs. I realized that not all parents were like mine, and there was actually something good in this world.

"Sister Thompson became my link to sanity, I think. She slipped me treats occasionally, and gave me a few dollars here and there when I got into junior high. She made certain that I got baptized. She had to argue with my father for over an hour to get his consent, even though he was technically a member of the Church. He'd never lived it. I think he was afraid of it.

"Anyway," Melody sighed, coming back to the present, "I guess I owe most of the credit to her. She was an incredible woman."

"Is she still around?"

"Oh, yes. I see her every week or two. She's ninety-one. Her sons keep close track of her, but she still lives in her own home. She was making a meat loaf the last time I stopped by."

"You know," Matthew said, "you can't give her all the credit." Melody looked baffled and he clarified, "She couldn't have made a difference if you'd stopped going to Primary like the rest of them."

Once again Melody tried to absorb a concept completely foreign to her. Not once, in all her years of struggling to rise above her past, had she considered that perhaps she was something special; that the reason she'd come this far was because of something divine inside herself.

"I have one more question," Matthew said, and Melody steeled herself for another uncomfortable inquiry about her family. But he only asked, "Does Sister Thompson like Christmas?"

Melody gave a disgusted laugh. "I suppose she does."

"And with all she did for you, she couldn't get *you* to like Christmas?"

"She's a nice old woman, not a miracle worker."

Matthew smiled, as if he'd told himself a secret. "Well, I'd like to meet her."

"Okay," Melody agreed. "That shouldn't be a problem."

"And then I'd like to meet your family."

Melody sighed. "Matthew, it has taken me a lot of soul searching, and prayer, and struggle to detach myself from my family. Every effort I have ever made to help any one of them has always resulted in disaster. I finally have my own place. They don't know my phone number. They don't know my address. They don't know where I work. And they don't know what kind of car I drive. I'd like to keep it that way. Because I learned a long time ago that if I could have fixed their problems, I would have. But I can't. So the best thing for all of us is for me to keep my distance."

Melody expected him to be somehow disgusted by her callousness toward her family. She was surprised when he said, "That is probably the most un-codependent thing I've ever heard anybody say."

After Melody digested the fact that she was talking to a man who even used the word *codependent* in his vocabulary, she absorbed a new twist on the fact that he had spent time working at a crisis center.

"What?" he asked when she said nothing more.

"I was just thinking that there's a remote possibility we could be compatible after all."

"Good, so take me to meet your family."

"Haven't you been listening to me?"

"Yes. I didn't say we had to engage in some welfare project. I just want to meet them."

"Well, my sisters probably aren't reachable. Lisa's in Mexico and Lydia's always with her boyfriend. And my brothers are probably drunk. Joe might still be in jail. Who knows?"

"Okay. But I can meet your mother. I just want to walk into your home and be introduced to your mother. It's not such a big deal."

"Okay, if you meet my mother, then we drop it."

"Fine," he said. Melody expected him to change the subject, but he added, "How about now? It's Sunday afternoon; we've got plenty of time. It shouldn't take long."

Melody was bombarded with memories of the countless times she had scrambled to make the front room barely presentable when she knew a date was coming to pick her up. She couldn't even imagine taking a man over there without a chance to buffer the reality. But what could she do? She didn't live there anymore, so she couldn't very well go over and start cleaning. Not that she'd want to.

"Okay, fine," she said. "But . . ."

"But what?" he urged.

Melody turned away, not wanting to admit to what she was thinking.

"What?" he persisted, touching her chin.

"I'm just so afraid that . . ." She turned away again when her voice cracked with emotion.

"What are you afraid of, Melody?"

"You know the truth about my family, but . . . but seeing it is entirely different. I'm just afraid that when you do . . . you'll . . ."

"What?" he pressed gently.

"I just don't want to lose you, Matthew." She looked up at him, huge tears brimming in her eyes.

Matthew kissed her quickly, saying, "I'm not going to judge you by your family, Melody."

"Well, maybe you should. Sometimes I'm not sure I have it in me to rise above it completely. It's like a ball and chain around my ankle. Dysfunctional people raise dysfunctional children, you know."

"Not when they have the strength to break those cycles and—"

"Well, maybe I'm not that strong!"

"Hey," Matthew spoke in a voice that calmed her, "I don't see a dysfunctional woman here. Beyond hating Christmas," he chuckled, "you seem to be functioning pretty well. As long as you're committed to the gospel and to rising above the past, I'm not the least bit concerned, Melody."

"Well, maybe you should be," she snapped. Then he kissed her and she had to smile. But in her heart she believed that once he saw the reality of what her home life had been like, he would change his mind.

Chapter Seven

Matthew stood up and held out a hand. "Come on," he said. "Let's go."

Melody sighed, resigning herself to the inevitable. "Okay, but let me call my mother first, and hope she doesn't slap me with some crisis she wants me to fix."

"You don't have to fix anything," he reminded her. "Just stick to your purpose."

Melody nodded and picked up the phone, praying inside that this would not turn out too horribly. She wished that Matthew wasn't listening when her mother answered.

"Hi, Mom. It's Melody."

"Oh, hi." Her mother sounded relatively cheerful and perky. So far, so good. "I must say I'm surprised to hear from you." There was a subtle bite in her statement, but Melody ignored it.

"Well, I just want to bring somebody over for a few minutes."

The silence on the other end of the phone betrayed her mother's surprise.

"We're going to go see Sister Thompson first. Could you please pick things up a little, okay?"

"Okay. Is it a man?"

"Yes, actually." She glanced at Matthew and smiled from his obvious pleasure. "It's a man."

"Oooh," Thelma Morgan drawled. "Is it serious?"

"I hope so, but . . . well, he wants to meet you. What happens beyond that is difficult to tell."

Matthew scowled at her and she turned her back to him, unable to handle the distraction.

"Mom, I know it's not easy for you, but could you ask the boys to behave? You know what I mean."

"I'll do my best, dear."

"Thanks. I'll see you in a while."

Melody hung up the phone and stared at it for a full minute.

"Hey, it'll be okay," Matthew said.

"Even if my brother's drunk and tells you to go to hell?"

"Would he do that?"

"Oh, would he!"

"I've been fairly warned. Come on, let's go."

Melody felt no apprehension at all as Matthew stopped the car in front of Sister Thompson's house. Even in the dead of winter her little yard looked immaculate. The same old wreath hung on the front door. Melody rang the bell, saying, "She's a little slow. It usually takes a few minutes."

Matthew smiled as if he was about to meet his favorite movie star or something. A meek voice called from the other side of the door, "Who is it?"

"It's Melody," she called back especially loud.

They could hear a lock turning, then the door opened wide. Matthew's first impression of Sister Thompson was the unmasked delight that shone from her aged face as she opened her arms to embrace Melody. Then her eyes shifted to Matthew.

"Oh, my," she said, taking Matthew's hand as she winked at Melody, "I've heard a lot about your boyfriends, but you've never brought one to meet me before. Come in. Come in. It's cold."

Matthew glanced around the small front room, absorbing its coziness. A small Christmas tree sat on a table in one corner, covered with decorations that could qualify as antiques. The Mormon Tabernacle Choir sang a popular Christmas carol from the little portable tape player sitting on an old-fashioned stereo cabinet. The room was tidy and full of the things that grandmothers collect. He turned his attention to Sister Thompson as Melody said loudly, "Matthew, this is Sister Thompson." She motioned toward him. "And this is Matthew Trevor."

"It's so good to meet you," the old woman beamed.

"And you," Matthew said as she motioned them toward the couch. She sat in a rocking chair to face them.

"I wanted to thank you," Matthew said, imitating Melody's voice level to accommodate the old woman's hearing.

"Thank me? For what?"

"For taking Melody to Primary."

The old woman laughed softly. "She's a wonderful girl, my Melody." She then turned to Melody and asked, "So, are you going to marry him?"

Melody glanced away with embarrassment. Matthew chuckled and answered, "If I can talk her into it. She's a little stubborn."

"You obviously know her well," Sister Thompson said. She went on to tell Matthew about her husband of fifty-seven years, who had passed away fourteen years earlier.

She recalled details of their early courtship and marriage with amazing detail, occasionally giggling as if the memories themselves still made her tingle.

Melody observed Matthew as Sister Thompson repeated stories that she had heard a dozen times. There was no hint of anything in Matthew's expression beyond absolute delight. The old woman eventually ran down with her stories and asked Matthew about himself. "Did you go on a mission?" she asked so forthrightly that again Melody chuckled from embarrassment.

But Matthew simply answered, "Yes I did. I went to Russia."

She asked him questions about the country and his experiences. She asked him about his family, then, "Are you going to school?"

"Yes. I'm attending Brigham Young University. I'm working toward a degree in law."

"Oooh," Sister Thompson drawled, looking at Melody as if to say, *What a fine catch*. Melody smiled at Matthew and relished the squeeze of his hand around hers. "And why law?" she asked.

"My father was a lawyer until last year when he became a judge," Matthew said. "His work has always inspired me. I hope to leave some degree of the mark on the world that he has."

As the conversation ran down, Melody's respite was dampened by the reality that they were going to her mother's house next. She longed to stay in the security of Sister Thompson's home, just as she had in her youth. Her visits here had always been a pleasant reprieve.

Sister Thompson thanked them over and over for their visit, and made them promise to let her know as soon as they set a date. Matthew told her with confidence that they would, while Melody found it difficult to believe such a thing was possible.

"Okay," Melody said when they were back in the car, "we can go back to your house now. Maybe we could watch one of those church videos you have, or even some silly Christmas movie. Or we could play a game with the kids or—"

"Where is it?" Matthew interrupted. "We don't have to stay long. It will be over in twenty minutes."

"Okay." She took a deep breath. "Four houses up, across the street. It's the one with the horrible yard and the chipping paint."

Matthew squeezed her hand, saying gently, "It's okay, Mel."

She nodded, but she didn't believe him. Her stomach was in knots and she felt her blood pressure rising.

Melody wouldn't normally knock at the door, but she did, hoping it would prompt some last-minute picking up. She pondered her mother's definition of "presentable," and the knot in her stomach tightened.

Her mother opened the door with a smile, actually looking pretty good. Melody wished they could just make introductions here and leave it at that.

"Hi," she said. "Come in."

As they stepped inside, Matthew was more preoccupied by the way Melody's hand tightened in his. He could feel cold sweat on her palm. He was oblivious to the quick appraisal she made of their surroundings as they entered.

Melody was relieved that the front room didn't look too bad. She knew by the smell of stale food that plates bearing the residue of yesterday's meals had been rushed to the kitchen following her call. Some odd pieces of silverware were still scattered on the end tables. The stacks of mail, newspapers, and magazines had been moved aside, and the center of the floor had been haphazardly vacuumed. A view of the kitchen table made it evident that the cleaning effort had not reached that far. Only one of her brothers was in the front room; that was only half the chance for trouble that two of them might make. The TV was on loud, playing a video tape of some movie—likely R-rated. Sounds of explosions and gunfire penetrated every corner of the room. The cigarette burning between her brother's fingers added a steady stream of smoke into the haze already present. The beer can in his hand wasn't a good sign, but it was no surprise.

Attempting to concentrate on her mother rather than her surroundings, Melody prompted herself to make introductions as quickly as possible. "Matthew, this is my mother, Thelma Morgan. Mother, this is Matthew Trevor."

Thelma wiped her hands on her pants, then extended one toward Matthew. He took her hand between both of his, holding it longer than necessary as he said, "It's a pleasure to meet you, Mrs. Morgan."

"Oh, and . . . you, too," she said, seeming flustered.

"And this is my brother, Ben," Melody added. Ben made no acknowledgment.

"Go ahead and sit down," Thelma said, motioning toward the couch.

Melody was about to say they couldn't stay when Matthew sat down. Thelma sat on one side of him, remaining at the edge of her seat, turning attentively toward him. Melody sighed and sat down on the other side, squeezing his hand tightly.

Thelma asked Matthew polite questions about his job and education. She was obviously impressed with his goal to become a lawyer, but she didn't seem interested in his family or religious convictions, as Sister Thompson had been.

"Well, we can't stay," Melody said, coming to her feet, wanting to get out before something awful happened.

Matthew stood beside her, saying, "It was good meeting you, Mrs. Morgan."

Thelma looked at Melody, then at him, saying tentatively, "So it must be serious, huh?"

"If we get married, we'll let you know," Melody said dryly. While she was contemplating a way to excuse themselves, a string of profanities erupted from the television. Melody squeezed her eyes shut, not even wanting to look at Matthew. She was ready to bolt out the door when her mother hollered at Ben. "Hey, turn that thing down and meet Melody's boyfriend."

Ben didn't respond and Thelma picked up the remote. As she paused the video, Ben looked up, his eyes angry and hard. Melody noted that he looked older every time she saw him. She wished they had left three minutes ago—or better yet, not come at all—as Ben yelled at Thelma in a voice so much like their father's that it made Melody's skin crawl. She wondered how a human being could manage to put four foul words into a twelve-word sentence with so little effort. She glanced at Matthew to gauge his reaction, and her heart fell to the pit of her stomach. The calm, confident expression he'd worn since they'd left his house was completely absent. She took his hand and hurried toward the door, calling over her shoulder, "It was good to see you, Mom. I'll keep you posted."

Thelma hollered something out the door, but Melody just waved and got into the car. As they drove away, she couldn't help noticing Matthew's mood. It was the first time she'd seen him so somber.

Unable to bear the silence, she said, "So, you've met them."

He nodded but didn't say anything. The knot in her stomach tightened. She noticed the smell of cigarette smoke hovering around them and felt nothing short of shame. How clearly she remembered having to go to school, and worse, church, smelling like she'd just emerged from a barroom. As she'd gotten older she had learned how to dress and behave in a way that allowed her to blend in, but the cigarette smoke was a dead giveaway that she was different from most of the children in a predominantly Mormon community.

The silence intensified as Matthew drove toward her apartment. She'd had the impression that he'd take her back to his house for a while. Had something changed? Were her fears a reality? Would he find a way to let her know that it just wasn't going to work out?

Matthew parked the car in front of her apartment, but he didn't get out. He'd always opened the door for her, so she assumed he wanted to talk. But he didn't.

"You're awfully quiet," she said.

Matthew turned to look at her, startled from the uneasiness hovering inside of him that he couldn't explain. He absorbed her expression and his thoughts shifted. She had told him of her upbringing, and he'd certainly never doubted it. But the reality was unsettling. He didn't know what to say, but his heartache on her behalf was almost unbearable. Impulsively he pulled her into his arms, holding her tightly, desperately, as if he could somehow shield her from the struggles of her past, and protect her from the remnants of it in the present.

Melody clung to Matthew, uncertain of his motives but comforted by the intensity of his embrace.

"I'm sorry," she whispered, if only to break the silence.

Matthew pulled back to look at her as if he had no idea what she was talking about. When it sank in, he asked, "What are *you* apologizing for? What exactly did you do wrong?"

Melody shook her head. "I don't know, Matthew. I think I've asked myself that question a million times. What did I do to deserve being born into a family like that?"

"I hope you realize that's not the way it works."

"Yes," her voice softened, "I know. Actually . . . my patriarchal blessing says I was so eager to come to earth that I was willing to take on any difficulty just to be here. I guess that puts it in a different perspective, but . . ." She stopped when it became evident that Matthew wasn't with her. His eyes had a subtle, glazed look that made her nervous. "What's wrong?" she demanded, startling him.

"I'm okay," he said.

"You're lying. I grew up with people who lie. I know when somebody's lying to me."

Matthew glanced away. "So I'm not okay, but . . . it's not what you think. I just . . ." Realizing the impression he was giving her, he said, "Listen, Melody, this has nothing to do with me and you."

"It most certainly does. That was my *family* back there. And you are obviously disturbed."

Matthew had to admit, "Yes, but . . . it's not about that. I . . ."

"You what?"

"I don't know how to explain it."

"Well, when you figure out how to explain it, you let me know. In the meantime, I'm just going to try to accept what I should have accepted from the start."

"And what is that?"

"You and I are from different worlds, Mr. Trevor. And

I'd be a fool to believe that someone like you would want to deal with a family like mine."

"You have no idea what you're talking about."

"Don't I? You have no idea what life is *really* like, Trevor. I might have grown up in *happy valley*, but it was still the ghetto."

"Do you know what you are?" he snapped. "You, Melody Morgan, are a snob! You're prejudiced and closed-minded toward anyone who didn't grow up the way you did. And that makes you a *snob*. Don't sit there and try to tell me what I'm feeling, and what I'm thinking, because you have no idea."

"So, tell me then, what exactly are you feeling?"

He sighed. "I . . . don't know. I need some time to—"

"Like I said, when you figure out how to explain it, you let me know." Melody got out of the car and slammed the door. Matthew knew he should go after her, but he didn't know what to say if he did. Right now he needed to be alone.

Driving toward home, the feeling intensified that had erupted during his encounter with Melody's brother. He could feel it, but he didn't understand it. It was as if a heavy mist stood between the emotion and being able to identify it.

Matthew went to his room when he got home, wanting only to be alone. He felt somehow scared and helpless, but he didn't understand why. Sitting on the floor, where he usually sat to unwind, Matthew thought through the scenario at Melody's house. Over and over the phrases catapulted through his head, while the uneasiness inside of him only increased. *Why?* He just didn't understand.

Turning his mind to prayer, Matthew begged for the Spirit's help in understanding. As he attempted to analyze his feelings, the answers came. But with them came an unexpected heartache. Pressing his head into his hands, Matthew unconsciously rocked back and forth. He was completely unaware of time passing; completely oblivious to his surroundings until his mother touched his shoulder and startled him. He gasped and looked into her eyes. She was kneeling beside him, tears running down her cheeks.

"Why are you crying?" he asked.

Janna wiped a hand over her face, saying, "I was about to ask you the same."

Matthew touched his face and found it wet. Had he been so lost in the memories that he hadn't even felt his own tears? He looked to his mother as if she might have the answer, but it was as if she'd seen a ghost. He was wondering how to ask what was wrong when she said, "What were you thinking about just now, Matthew? You seemed a million miles away . . . or maybe just twenty years or so."

Matthew took a sharp breath, wondering how his mother had guessed that his mind had been absorbed in memories of his early childhood. Was that the reason for her tears?

"I haven't seen you like this since . . ." Her voice trailed off.

"Like what?" he demanded.

"Rocking like that . . . with your hands over your ears."

Just hearing the description seemed to intensify memories that he wasn't prepared to deal with.

"What happened to bring this on, Matthew? Does it have something to do with Melody?"

He nodded. "I made her take me to meet her family. And . . . at first I didn't understand why it made me so uncomfortable. But now I know."

"Tell me," she urged.

"It was . . ." His voice cracked. ". . . The way her brother spoke to her mother. His tone of voice; the things he said. It was just like . . ." Matthew pressed his face to his mother's shoulder and cried like a child. When he calmed down he had to admit, "I thought I'd dealt with all of that. I thought it was behind me, but . . ."

"You dealt with it fairly well, Matthew. But it hasn't come up since that incident just before your mission. My guess is that you dealt with it as a child, and you understood a little more the last time it came up. But you've never looked at it from the perspective of being an adult. I'm no psychologist, but I have a little experience in such things. I would bet that once you take it out and look at it, you'll be able to put it behind you with more understanding and maturity."

Matthew thought about that. It made sense. And it made him feel a little better. But he had to ask, "Was it as bad as I'm remembering? Sometimes it just seems like a bad dream."

"It was a nightmare, Matthew. It was a living hell. And I thank God every day that you and I were able to escape when we did."

Matthew held his mother close to him, the way he'd always wanted to as a child. He'd wanted to protect her and keep her safe, but he'd been helpless to do anything about it at the time.

For more than an hour, Matthew and his mother talked about the disturbing incidents from his childhood. Thinking of Melody, there was one point that troubled him. "Mom," he asked, "do you think I have what it takes to help Melody rise above her upbringing? Am I strong enough to—"

"Matthew," she took his hand, "there is only one way to be certain if she's the right one for you, and that is to take it to the Lord. But from what little I've observed, I think the two of you are a good match. While you're thinking it through, weigh the possible outcome of your choices. Would you want Melody to marry a man who had no idea how she felt, or what she'd been through?"

Matthew had to admit that his mother's question struck him deeply. It was nearly eleven o'clock before he finally came to terms with what had happened to him today. And he knew he'd never sleep until he talked to Melody. He nearly called her, but it wasn't good enough. Driving to her apartment, the emotion struck him all over again. But he felt immensely grateful for the understanding and insight he'd found. He couldn't comprehend attempting to deal with such things without the gospel. He only hoped he could make Melody understand.

* * * * *

Melody lay staring into the darkness above her. She'd gone to bed almost as soon as Matthew had brought her home. At first she'd tried with everything she had to not think about it. But eventually the reality crowded everything else away, and she'd cried until her tears gave way to a familiar numbness. She loved Matthew Trevor. And she was afraid she'd lost him.

A pounding at the door startled her. She glanced at the clock. It was well past eleven.

"Who in the world," she murmured, reaching for her bathrobe. On first impulse she thought it was one of her siblings; it was their style to bang on the door at all hours. But she'd been so careful about keeping her address a secret.

"Who is it?" she called, flipping on the light.

"It's Matthew," he called back.

Melody hated her heart for the way it began to pound as she unlocked the door and pulled it open. She felt suddenly uncomfortable as they stood face to face, knowing he couldn't help but see that she'd been crying. She motioned him inside and closed the door. As he turned to look at her again, she gasped softly. It was evident that he'd been crying, too. She wondered how hard a man had to cry for his eyes to be that red and puffy.

"Are you okay?" she asked, her heart quickening. Had he come to tell her that it just wasn't going to work out? Was his emotion the result of coming to terms with the obvious glitch in their relationship? Had he realized that the package she would bring into his life was simply not something he wanted to deal with?

Matthew glanced away, not certain where to begin now that he was here. The discomfort he'd felt earlier rushed in all over again.

"Matthew." She nudged him when he didn't answer.

"Uh . . . I'm sorry to wake you. I just . . . had to talk to you, and . . ."

"You didn't wake me," she insisted. "Sit down."

Matthew sat on one of the kitchen chairs and leaned his elbows on the table. "There's something I need to tell you, but it's not easy to talk about, so. . . be patient with me."

"I'm listening," she said, but her tone was colored with the same defensiveness he'd sensed earlier.

"When we left your mother's house earlier," he began, "I felt very uncomfortable, I admit. After what you'd told me about your family, what I saw didn't surprise me. And it didn't make me think any less of you. But it did trigger something in me; something that's difficult for me to explain, and . . ."

"If you're trying to tell me you can't live with it, just say so and get it over with. It wouldn't be the first time I've been dumped because—"

"Stop that!" Matthew grasped her shoulders. "You don't even know what you're talking about. Just stop your self-righteous assumptions long enough to hear what I have to say."

"It doesn't matter how you say it, Matthew, the facts don't change. If you—"

"Listen to me!" he shouted, and Melody was stunned into silence. There was nothing she hated more than an angry man. She'd spent her life listening to drunken rages—first her father; then her brothers. Now she steeled herself to escort Matthew to the door if he so much as raised his voice one more decibel. The intensity in his eyes deepened, and she felt herself tightening up inside. But his voice became low and gravelly as he muttered, "This isn't about you, Melody. It's *me*. Do you hear what I'm saying? It's *me.*"

"Oh, *you* have a problem, because you can't handle—"

Matthew pressed his mouth over hers just long enough to stop her ranting. Then he drew back only far enough to see her eyes. "Now, be quiet long enough for me to say what I have to say. I didn't come here to tell you it's over, unless you can't handle having a man who reverts to his childhood when he hears your brother shouting."

Melody opened her mouth, but no sound came out. Matthew's voice deepened with emotion, and tears brimmed in his eyes. "It happened when Ben yelled at your mother—the things he called her, that tone of voice. I thought I'd dealt with it. I thought I'd risen above it. But I went home and curled up on the floor and cried like a baby, because that's how my stepfather talked to my mother . . . only it was worse; so much worse. I learned to shut it all out, but I realized today that it's still there. It was like a switch went on in my head and I could hear the vile, filthy things he'd say to her. I could hear her screaming, fighting him off. And when she was bruised and battered, she'd get up to fix the meals and clean the house to avoid another beating. And she'd smile at me with bruises on her face and tell me everything was going to be all right. And I'd have to lie to her and tell her that he'd never hurt me, because he swore he'd kill her if I ever told anybody. I realized much later that on the days when she couldn't get out of bed at all, she was miscarrying babies because of the abuse. When we finally got away, leaving practically everything behind, I was the happiest kid in the world. Then one day he found us. I ran in the bedroom to hide, the way I always had. And I called the police; otherwise he *would* have killed her. She spent weeks in the hospital. And for a long time I truly believed he had done that to her because *I* had told the truth about what he'd done to me."

Matthew finished with a stilted sob. *"That's* what happened inside of me today, Melody. It has *nothing* to do with you. But, in my opinion, it's one damn good reason why you and I should be together."

After Melody digested the fact that she wasn't the only Mormon who occasionally cussed out loud, she attempted to absorb what he'd just told her. Tears trickled down her face. She shook her head, attempting to let him know she was too overcome to speak. But he obviously misinterpreted as he sputtered, "Don't you see, Melody? You and I understand each other. It's almost as if your spirit cried out to me the first time I saw you; like something intangible told me we were two of a kind."

Melody only shook her head again. She was so stunned, so overwhelmed, that her thoughts wouldn't even come together in any recognizable form. She only knew that she loved him more than ever before.

Chapter Eight

As Melody just stared into Matthew's eyes, something inside her changed. She had always believed that eventually she could overcome her hang-ups and make a relationship with any man who loved her and was truly committed. But she had never dreamed of finding a man who might actually *know* how she felt. The men she knew who came from abusive backgrounds were still wallowing in the muck. But here before her was tangible evidence that abuse and dysfunction could be overcome. Here was a man who had experienced the horrors of abuse, yet he had risen above it. He was strong in the gospel, capable of functioning in a real family, with real values, and he had the ability to achieve his goals.

With no words spoken, she felt as if their spirits somehow connected in that moment. Or perhaps it was as Matthew had said: maybe they had connected the moment they'd first met. She had just been too caught up in her pride and fears to see it. She didn't know whether to laugh or cry as he stood and opened his arms, silently inviting her to accept him for who he was, and allow him to do the same for her. Melody clung to him and sobbed with laughter. The way he held her made her believe in miracles. She was realistic enough to know that struggles were a part of life, and she would likely have more than her share. But with a man like Matthew Trevor, she truly believed she could take on the world and win.

When her emotion settled, she and Matthew sat close together on the couch and talked until two in the morning. He went home with a kiss at the door, and she felt compelled to finally admit, "I love you, Matthew." He grinned like a child, and Melody went to bed happier than she'd ever been in her life.

The next few days, she hardly saw Matthew for a minute. He was studying for finals and working long hours, but he called her every day and told her he'd pick her up Thursday afternoon when she got off work.

Melody was full of butterflies when Thursday came. Life almost felt too good to be true. She glanced at the video store clock, pleasantly surprised that the time had gone quickly. Matthew would be here any minute to get her. They were going Christmas shopping for his family, and she wasn't even dreading it. With Matthew in her life, she was beginning to believe that she could even endure Christmas.

She buttoned up her coat and walked outside, almost running into Matthew. "Hello, gorgeous," he said, kissing her quickly and taking her hand.

"Hello," she replied, unable to keep from grinning.

He smirked at her as they walked toward the car.

"What?" she asked.

"I just thought you'd be all depressed and uptight, since we're doing *you know what,*" he whispered.

"I'm fine, really."

"Oooh, I think we're making progress."

"Maybe we are."

Matthew looked up as he turned the key in the car door to see a young woman approaching. Her appearance, along with her determined expression, made him suddenly nervous. He almost expected her to pull out a switchblade and demand their valuables.

Melody glanced up when Matthew hesitated to open the door. "Oh, help," she muttered and turned the other direction to steel herself.

"What?" he asked.

"That's my sister."

"Really?"

Melody frowned at his obvious delight. He absorbed the young woman all over again. Her hair was colored an unnatural red and starched into a ridiculous style. Her clothes were dark and baggy. She had more pieces of hardware in her ears than he could count, and a silver stud piercing the side of her nose. She had the appearance of a teenager, with eyes that looked old and haggard. And she was very pregnant. It was difficult not to be intrigued by the contrast between these sisters. He was amazed at how two women could turn out so differently, growing up in the same home. If nothing else, this was tangible evidence of Melody's inner strength.

"What are you doing here?" Melody asked firmly, but with no sign of malice. "I asked you not to bother me at work."

"I didn't bother you. I waited until you came out. And it wasn't easy finding you."

"That's the idea," Melody countered.

"Mom said you wouldn't even leave her your new phone number."

Melody diverted the topic. "I assume you need something."

Matthew felt himself being surveyed as Melody's sister seemed to just now grasp the fact that they weren't alone. She looked him up and down, smiling in a way that made him almost feel defiled. But he just smiled.

As Melody observed the silent exchange between Matthew and her sister, she resigned herself to introductions. "This is Matthew, a very good friend. Matthew, my sister, Lydia."

Matthew extended a hand without hesitation. "It's a pleasure to meet you, Lydia."

"Oooh," Lydia said more to Melody, "and he's a real gentleman, just like Mom said. But she didn't mention how adorable he is. How did you get so lucky?"

Matthew sensed Melody's irritation and embarrassment. He put an arm possessively around her shoulders, saying with a grin, "If there's any luck, it's mine."

Melody glanced up at Matthew in disbelief. Lydia looked somehow irritated.

"We have an appointment," Melody said to her sister, hoping she'd get to the point. She could feel it coming. One way or another, their encounters always had something to do with Lydia's lack of financial resources.

"Listen," Lydia lowered her voice as if she didn't want to be overheard, "I know you told me you wouldn't loan me any more money, but . . ." She glanced at Matthew again as if she wished he wasn't there. But he didn't move.

"But?" Melody pressed.

"I'm about to have a baby, for crying out loud. Couldn't you just—"

"There are programs available to cover all of your medical expenses, Lydia."

"I know. And I'm doing that, but—"

"But what?"

"I have to eat."

"There are programs available that provide food, as well."

"Yes, but, there are just little things that—"

"You know, you could probably even get a job if you'd clean yourself up a little."

"And how am I supposed to work with a baby?"

Melody ignored that one. The baby was just one more excuse to avoid responsibility. "I assume from past experience that what you're really in need of is cold, hard cash. Like the money you took out of my purse the last time I helped you. A ride, you wanted. Just a ride. I still don't know how you managed to clean me out. Did you do it while I was pumping gas? I couldn't even afford a bus fare after Joe wrecked my car. Every step I took in the cold, I thought of you."

"Oh, lighten up, Mel."

"By lighten up, do you mean hand over money for beer and cigarettes? I know it frustrates you that the government doesn't have programs to cover *that,* but I think you're going to have to learn to live with it."

"Just loan me ten or twenty dollars."

"Loan?" Melody actually laughed. "If you had ever paid back even a dime of everything I had *loaned* to you before now, maybe we could talk about it."

"I will." Lydia's agitation increased. She was obviously desperate, and almost shaking. "When I get back on my feet and—"

"Lydia, I've been hearing that for years. I know it must be terribly difficult for you to have to come and ask me for money when you know I can't give it to you. If you really want to get back on your feet, take that ring out of your nose

99

and go to church. *They* have the means to help you. *I* don't."

Lydia muttered a few profanities directed at her sister, ending with, "You think religion can solve everything."

"Yes, I do," Melody said without apology. She wanted to just get away, but she had to ask, "When's the baby due?"

"Next month some time, I think." Lydia obviously didn't want to talk about that.

"And its father?"

"He's . . . around."

"Lydia," Melody felt suddenly desperate herself, "there's one thing I'll help you with."

"Oh, not this again," Lydia snarled, but Melody ignored her.

"Let me help you find somebody to raise the baby. You're not ready to be a mother."

Again Lydia got angry, accusing Melody of finding a perverse pleasure in seeing the government take away their older sister's children, accusing her of wanting to see Lydia in ruin, of wanting to take away the only thing that meant something to her.

"Get me out of here," Melody whispered to Matthew.

He hurried to open the car door, and she got in and locked it.

"It was a pleasure, Lydia," Matthew said with a smile that apparently took her so off guard that she stopped shouting. "Take care now."

Matthew got in and drove away, not surprised by the tears running down Melody's cheeks. "You okay?" he asked, pressing her hand briefly to his lips.

"You know," she said, dabbing at her eyes with a napkin she'd pulled out of her purse, "I always believed she had a strong spirit. I thought there was something inside of her that wouldn't go so low. And I wonder where that went. I get so *angry* with her, and at the same time . . . I want so badly to just put my arms around her and love her."

"But she won't let you."

Melody shook her head. "Maybe it's because she's the younger one; maybe I feel more responsible for her than the others. I'd like to help them all, but . . ." Her emotion intensified. "But I can't."

"You handled her very well," he said. "You were strong and firm without getting angry. I was impressed."

Melody chuckled through a sob. "Yeah, that's why she was screaming at me. It's so touching when your siblings call you a . . . never mind."

"I know what you mean."

"I've considered just moving far away, but a part of me feels like I need to be close by for my mother. I prayed about it and knew it was right to not give her my phone number, but I felt as if the Spirit told me I would know if I was needed. I know I can't do anything for my brothers and sisters. But my heart aches for that baby, Matthew. When there are so many people out there desperately trying to adopt babies, why do girls like Lydia have to be so determined to keep them at all costs? If the child even survives physically, can you imagine the damage she will do to it emotionally? And spiritually, I don't even want to think—"

She couldn't go on as emotion overcame her. Matthew held her hand as she looked out the window and cried. She was surprised when he pulled into a parking lot nowhere near their destination. He put the car in park and turned to pull her into his arms. He just held her until she calmed down, then he handed her another napkin and assured her it would be all right.

Melody managed to enjoy their excursion to the mall, but thoughts spurred by her sister's appearance hovered with her far into the night. She prayed to find peace and turned her thoughts to images she had conjured up as a child to get her through the most difficult times.

How could she ever forget the time she'd shown up at Sister Thompson's house, fighting back her emotion, not wanting her kind friend to see it? She couldn't have been more than nine. Sitting in Primary that day, she remembered wanting to absorb everything around her, but her mind was clouded with memories of her father's drunken rage that had kept them all awake until four in the morning, when he'd finally passed out. Melody had hardly slept at all, afraid that he would wake up again. She wondered what else he might break, who he might hit next. She managed to maintain her composure through the meeting—until singing time started out with *I Am a Child of God*. How could she even put a voice to those words? . . . *With parents kind and dear*.

Everything blurred as her eyes filled with hot tears. And the next thing she knew, Sister Thompson was leading her into the hall. She led Melody into a vacant classroom and closed the door. "Just go ahead and cry, honey," she said, holding her close. And Melody did just that. When she had calmed down, Sister Thompson told her a story. Melody couldn't remember it exactly, but she knew it was about heroes and angels, and it had something to do with the Book of Mormon. And Melody felt better.

When Primary was over, Sister Thompson asked Melody to come to her house for a while. She called Melody's mother and was given permission to have the girl for the afternoon. They ate some soup and crackers together, then Sister Thompson told her more stories about heroes and angels. Melody didn't know how it applied to her, but she liked the pictures in Sister Thompson's Book of Mormon that went along with the stories. She'd heard them before, but she'd never comprehended until then that they were about real people. And even though the pictures were only an artist's interpretation of how they might have looked, the images helped Melody imagine them more clearly.

She became even more attentive when Sister Thompson told her a story about a righteous man who had lived not so many years ago. He had seen a vision of Nephite warriors guarding a temple to keep the evil spirits away. Then she described a similar image to Melody. "Next time you're afraid, honey, you just imagine one of these heroes standing guard at your bedroom door. I know that angels are real, child. I've felt their presence in my life."

Melody's eyes widened. "Do they have wings?" she asked.

Sister Thompson smiled. "No, honey. The wings are only a symbol. When we see angels with wings, it only reminds us that they are heavenly messengers. Angels are nothing more or less than people like you and me who are on the other side of the veil. They are always close, even though we can't see them. All of the heroes in these stories are now angels, and they can watch over you. All you have to do is ask your Father in Heaven to send an angel. You won't be able to see him, but if you try really hard to have faith, you'll be able to feel him close by. It's not always a very strong feeling, but it's there nevertheless."

"Is it like the way I felt after I was baptized?"

"Yes, honey. That's what it's like."

Melody liked Sister Thompson's theory on heroic angels. She read and reread the stories in her Book of Mormon that the older woman had helped her mark. Captain Moroni defeating the wicked Lamanites. Mormon leading armies into battle as a young man. Another Moroni who kept himself hidden from the Lamanites in order to complete the record and bury it. Nephi subduing his older brothers; she liked that one especially.

With a vivid imagination, Melody conjured up an image of her own hero. He was somehow a combination of several personages: tall and firm and strong, dressed like a warrior, complete with shield and sword. His features and coloring were obscure, but his image was strong. From then on, when her father would rage and throw his drunken fits, while her mother cried and groveled to defend herself, Melody imagined her angel warrior standing in the doorway of the room she shared with her sisters. Sometimes he would stand right at the foot of her bed. And Sister Thompson had been right; Melody never really saw him, but she felt him there without question.

When Melody was a young teenager, Sister Thompson had taken her to the Church Distribution Center. They looked at many wonderful things, but Melody was drawn to the large pictures of all the heroes she'd read about. She was surprised to realize that anyone could buy them. Sister Thompson told her she could pick out her two favorites, and she would buy them for Melody.

It took a long time for Melody to decide. They were all so wonderful. She asked Sister Thompson questions about each one. She liked the one of Nephi subduing his brothers. She liked Captain Moroni holding the Title of Liberty. She liked Helaman, sitting on his horse, leading the stripling warriors into battle. But she finally settled on two pictures that somehow helped close the distance between heroes and angels. The first was Moroni burying the plates. His hair was gray, but his face was rugged and masculine; his arms were tight with muscles as he laid his hands on the golden plates with his face lifted heavenward in prayer. The other picture was the same Moroni, as an angel, standing in the air above Joseph Smith's bed. With the two side by side, she could see both the man and the angel, and it was easier than ever to imagine her angel hero standing guard at the foot of her bed.

Melody was a woman now. The gospel had literally been the iron rod that had enabled her to rise above her past and find peace through righteous living. Her father was long dead, and to this day she could find no grief. But she'd stopped feeling guilty for that, and she'd stopped feeling accountable for her family members. She knew in her heart that it was beyond her capacity to help them. She put their names on temple prayer rolls regularly. She prayed for them herself. She asked the Lord to help her know if she was needed. And that was all she could do. The one thing she hadn't mastered was not caring. No matter how she tried, she couldn't free herself of the heartache.

Melody finally drifted to sleep with images of her angel hero standing at the foot of her bed, protecting her from the horrors of the world, assuring her that she'd done her best. His presence alone reminded her of God's love. He was, after all, a heavenly messenger.

She awoke when the alarm went off, smacked it, then sank back into her pillow, longing for more sleep. As she lay half awake, trying to talk herself into getting up, she saw an image in her mind as clearly as if it was a photograph. It only lasted a moment, but its impression was remarkable.

Melody turned over and looked around her, as if there might be some explanation. She might have thought it had only been her imagination, except that she hadn't been thinking about her angel hero at all. But she had seen him in her mind's eye, standing above her, as if he was a few rungs higher on some kind of ladder. With both arms outstretched, he had taken hold of her hands to lift her up. It was as simple as that. And the thought warmed her.

Matthew called a few minutes before she left for work. "I just wondered if you're all right," he said with such sincerity that she was almost moved to tears.

"I'm fine, really," she said. But she felt certain that he suspected how difficult her encounter with Lydia had been.

"You have a good day," he said. "I'll see you tomorrow."

"I can't wait," she admitted.

"What do you want to do?"

"I don't care," she said. "I just want to be with you."

Matthew laughed as if he was the happiest man alive.

Melody felt cheerful and content as she went to work. The image of her little *vision* of her angel hero hovered with her through the day, becoming more clear in her memory. If she closed her eyes to think about it, she could almost feel the tight grip of his hands around hers.

The work day was long, since she was doing a double shift, having traded with another employee so she could have tomorrow off. But she didn't feel tired or discouraged. She was looking forward to being with Matthew, and she felt the presence of her angel hero nearby.

Chapter Nine

Saturday morning arrived with heavy gray clouds. But Melody was so happy to be with Matthew that she didn't even complain about helping him finish his Christmas shopping. He took her to lunch, then they went to his house where she helped him wrap gifts in his bedroom.

"Hey," he said when they were finally finished and he lay back on the floor, "have you read that book yet?"

Melody scowled at him, then continued cleaning up the scraps of wrapping paper. "No, I haven't had time."

"You just don't want to read it."

"Whatever gave you that idea?" she asked with sarcasm.

Matthew turned on his side and leaned his head into his hand. His eyes turned serious. "I wanted you to read it before we see the movie. It's my favorite."

Rather than arguing with him, she asked, "And why is that?"

"Why?" he chuckled. "It's just so . . . good. Do you have any idea how much impact that one story has had on mankind? I *know* it was divinely inspired. It's all about . . . change of heart. You know, Alma talks about that in the Book of Mormon. In fact, most of the really good

Christmas stories are about change of heart. If you won't read *A Christmas Carol,* at least read what Alma has to say about it, okay?"

"I've read it. . . several times."

"Well, read it again . . . and this time, try to apply it to Christmas, okay?"

Melody sighed and shook her head. "What makes you think you could spend the rest of your life with someone like me?"

"The rest of my life?" he retorted. "Either it's forever, or it's not at all."

"Okay, *forever.* If you love things I hate, how can we possibly make it through forever? Do you think you can just step into my life and change who I am?"

"Melody," he took her hand, "I am *not* trying to change who you are. I just want *you* to find out who you are. I want nothing more than to help you get past all the hurt and just find the real you."

Melody was so touched she didn't know what to say. She settled for a simple, "I love you, Matthew Trevor."

"I know," he smirked. "Enough to read that book?"

Melody smiled. "Maybe."

A quick knock at the door preceded Matthew's father sticking his head in. "There you are," Colin said. "Could I get you to do something for me?"

"Sure," Matthew said without hesitation.

"There's something wrong with one of the light sets on the roof. Would you check it out?"

"On second thought," Matthew teased, "I think I'm busy. Isn't crawling around on rooftops a Santa Claus thing?"

"Yeah, well," Colin said, "he's not here right now, and you're a lot younger and more agile than I am."

"I'll do it," Matthew laughed. "I'm just giving you a hard time."

"Thank you," Colin said, then his eyes focused on Melody. "How are you today, young lady?"

"I'm fine, how are you?" she replied.

"Getting better all the time," he said and left the room.

"Better than what?" Melody asked after Colin was gone.

Matthew smiled. "Oh, he always says that."

Melody stood by the back porch in the dusky evening light while Matthew climbed up a sturdy trellis and onto the roof. He peered down at her and she hollered, "You're pretty good at that. Maybe you *are* Santa Claus. That's it, isn't it? You're actually the real jolly old elf in disguise, and you're determined to torture me through the entire Christmas season. Then you'll disappear and go back to the North Pole."

"If only you could be so lucky," he laughed. "Come on up." He motioned with his arm.

"Oh, no. I don't like to climb."

"Oh, come on. If you never make the climb, you'll never be able to see the view."

"Oh, now you're a philosopher."

Matthew laughed. "Better that than Santa Claus. You're trying to change the subject."

"Yes, I am."

"Come up here, Melody Noel, or I'm coming down to get you."

"Okay, fine," she snarled and started carefully up the trellis. The last step looked awfully far from the roof once she got there. She looked up at Matthew, suddenly afraid, ready to go back down. He lay on his belly and held both hands down toward her, saying gently, "Just hold on tight. I won't let you fall."

Melody inhaled deeply. She took hold of one hand, then the other. With her hands wrapped tightly in his, Matthew lifted her onto the roof. Melody forgot she was afraid as she suddenly felt like she'd done this before. While she was trying to pass it off as nothing, the memory of her angel hero flashed into her mind. She would never forget the momentary vision she'd had of him taking both her hands and lifting her upward.

Matthew came to his feet with her hands still in his. Melody found her footing on the shingles and looked up into his eyes. She didn't fully understand what had just happened, but she couldn't deny the emotion filling her.

Matthew became alarmed when Melody's eyes filled with tears that quickly fell down her face. "What is it?" he asked gently.

She smiled serenely and shook her head, saying only, "Let's get those lights fixed, shall we?"

They talked and laughed, pulling out every bulb in the faulty light set until they found the guilty one and replaced it. Together they laughed as it lit up. "Just in time," Matthew said. "Another five minutes and we wouldn't be able to see." He sat on the roof and urged Melody beside him, putting his arm around her. They sat in peaceable silence as darkness settled in over the neighborhood and the houses lit up in a variety of twinkling Christmas lights.

"It's beautiful," she said. "Everything looks so peaceful from up here."

"Yes, it does." Matthew touched her chin, tilting her face toward his. Melody held her breath as he meekly touched his lips to hers. "I love you," he whispered, pressing his forehead to hers.

"I love you, too," she replied, and he wrapped her tightly in his arms.

"Why were you crying?" he asked, almost expecting her to become tense. But she softened in his embrace and laid her head against his shoulder, sighing contentedly.

"It's hard to explain," she said. "Or maybe it's kind of a secret."

Matthew looked into her eyes. The Christmas lights surrounding them on the roof reflected off her face. He was dying of curiosity, but she only said, "I just think my Father in Heaven might be trying to tell me something."

"And what might that be?"

Melody touched his face. "That you're the best thing that ever happened to me."

"And that's why you were crying?"

"Sort of. But . . . it's more to do with angels, I think."

"Christmas angels?"

"Warrior angels," she replied, gratified by his increasing interest. Then she smiled. "But then . . . an angel is an angel, isn't it?"

He chuckled. "I don't have any idea what you're talking about."

"Well, maybe one day I'll tell you."

"Yeah," he chuckled. "Like you're going to read that book?"

"Maybe."

Matthew lifted his brows comically and kissed her again with a hint of passion seeping through.

"I love the way you kiss me," she said.

"Really?"

"Oh, yes. Maybe it's because no one has ever kissed me that way before."

"And how is that?" He sounded amused.

"Well . . . it's difficult to explain. Maybe it's because the guys who showed an interest in me were always . . ."

"What?" he asked when she stopped.

Melody hadn't intended to get into a detailed explanation, but they didn't seem to be in any hurry. Even the cold seemed insignificant as they held each other close.

"Well, when you go to school smelling like cigarette smoke, and wearing hand-me-downs, you just attract certain types of people. I never really had close friends. I wouldn't get involved in the things those kinds of people got involved in, and the good kids wouldn't hang around with me because of my background. I mean, would you want your kids spending time with someone who had people living at her house who were usually drunk and regularly went in and out of jail?

"Anyway," she continued, amazed at Matthew's attentiveness, "I just never seemed to get asked out by guys who had any morals. A kiss was always something cheap. It was just a physical thing. And once I got kissed, it seemed I had to fight to keep their hands off me. Finally, I just quit dating. Since I got out on my own, it hasn't been so bad. But I just haven't found anyone worth going out with twice. Somehow I got through all of that unscathed . . . physically, anyway."

"It's admirable, Melody."

"I don't know about that." She shook her head, then she looked at him again. "I only know that when you kiss me, I feel nothing but loved and respected." Her voice became dreamy. "It's incredible."

Matthew kissed her again as if to demonstrate her theory. He pressed his fingers into her hair. Their kiss lengthened, becoming warm and searching, but it never lost that magical quality she had just described. She could spend the rest of her life just being kissed by Matthew Trevor.

* * * * *

When the weekend was over, Melody felt a cloud descend over her. It was difficult to go back to work, knowing she wouldn't see Matthew as often. He was finishing up finals and working long hours for the Christmas rush so he could have extra time off during the holidays. But Melody knew her discouragement went much deeper than missing Matthew. Christmas was less than a week away, and in spite of all Matthew's efforts to get her to see the good in Christmas, she just couldn't. Oh, she'd felt glimpses of it. But it was as if having been exposed to what Christmas was supposed to be like actually deepened the heartache when she thought of all she'd missed. No matter how she tried, she just couldn't free herself from the shackles of her past. Each time she tried to imagine herself in a setting where Christmas celebrations and evidence of a good life surrounded her, thoughts of her family crept in to shatter the image. She began to doubt her ability to give Matthew the love he deserved. Yes, they shared some things in common by virtue of the abuse in their childhoods. But he'd been raised in a loving home since that time. On one hand she could tally the evidence that they were right for each other, and she couldn't deny the love she felt for him. But on the other hand, it was difficult to imagine herself having what it took to make a man like him happy.

* * * * *

Late Sunday evening, Matthew asked his mother if she'd have time to do some shopping with him the following morning.

"I'd love to, Matthew. But tomorrow's just too full. Can we go Tuesday?"

"Well . . . tomorrow's Melody's birthday. I was hoping for a woman's opinion."

"I'll go," Caitlin volunteered.

"Yeah, me too," Mallory added.

"It looks like you've got a woman's opinion," Janna said.

Having the assistance of his teenage sisters wasn't exactly what Colin had had in mind, but he gladly accepted their company as he went shopping Monday morning.

"Okay, where to?" he asked.

"The Dollar Store," they said in unison.

"I don't think that—"

"Trust us, Matthew," Caitlin insisted. "We have an idea, and we talked to Mom about it. Trust us."

Matthew sighed and drove the car to The Dollar Store. He pushed the cart through the store while his sisters filled it with an odd array of things. They made a few more stops, then they went back to the house. Matthew mostly watched as his sisters donated a large wicker basket to the cause. They crumpled colored tissue paper to fill in the bottom, then artistically arranged all the little things they'd purchased. They finished by tying a big bow and some helium balloons to the basket handle. And Matthew had to admit, "You're right. It's great."

They begged to go with him to deliver it, but he insisted that it was a man's job, and it had to be done without his little sisters in tow. "But," he added on his way out the door, "I'll be back in a while, and you can help me with another project . . . if you're not too busy."

* * * *

Melody went through the motions of going to work Monday morning, but in her heart she felt more Scroogey than she ever had in her life. She attempted to concentrate on the computer screen behind the desk, but it was difficult to even keep her thoughts straight while her emotions were all tangled in knots. Hearing one of her fellow employees gasp, she looked up to see Matthew entering the store, his face partially obscured by a basket and balloons. "Oh, my gosh," she muttered, and didn't know whether to laugh or cry.

He set the basket on the counter and leaned over to kiss her cheek. "I heard it was your birthday."

Melody couldn't even find her voice.

"What's wrong?"

"I honestly forgot it was my birthday."

"Well, now you remember."

The emotion Melody had been fighting forced its way to the surface. Matthew looked alarmed as she pressed a hand over her mouth and turned away. "Melody," he whispered, "it's just a birthday present."

"I know," she managed, aware of everyone in the store watching her—employees and customers alike. "Let's get out of here." She turned to one of the other employees standing close by and said, "I'm taking my lunch break now."

"Okay," she answered. "Happy birthday!" she hollered as Melody walked toward the door with Matthew and his basket.

Matthew opened the car door for Melody and stuffed the basket and balloons in the backseat. She said nothing as they drove.

"Did I do something wrong?" he finally asked.

"No, of course not," she insisted. "It's just that . . ."

"What?"

"I've never had a birthday present . . . or balloons . . . or . . . oh, you big creep!" she cried, frantically wiping at her tears. "Why do you have to do this to me?"

Matthew couldn't tell if she was teasing or not. "Where do you want to go?" he asked.

"I want to go home and fix my makeup."

When they got to her apartment, Matthew set the basket on the table while Melody went into the bathroom. When she came out, he couldn't tell if she was pleased or not, and he wondered what to say. Without a word she pushed her arms around him and held him tightly. He returned her embrace and pressed his lips into her hair.

"I didn't intend to upset you, Melody. If I embarrassed you, or—"

"No, it's not that. I mean . . ." She stepped back and motioned toward the basket. "It's so neat," she said, and started to cry again.

"What's wrong?" he asked.

"I don't know," she snapped. "Maybe it's PMS."

"Or maybe it's PCS," he countered. She looked baffled and he said, "Pre-Christmas Syndrome."

Her eyes smiled. "Or maybe it's both."

Melody took a deep breath and surveyed Matthew's gift. "This is incredible," she said.

"I owe most of the credit to my sisters," he said.

"I'll have to be sure and thank them."

One by one, Melody took the items out of the basket and set them on the table. There were candles, pencils, and magnets for her refrigerator. She found earrings, which she actually liked, and fingernail polish. There were pens, and paper clips, and a little stuffed animal. There was soap that smelled good, bath oil, bath salts, and bath gel. There was hair spray, hair gel, hair mousse, and shampoo. She found candy bars and kitchen gadgets. And at the bottom she found a birthday card. She looked tentatively at Matthew as she broke the seal on the envelope. "It's a *Hallmark,*" she said.

"Yeah, I bought it at that store you hate to go into."

"Well, the next time I go in there, I'll remember being there with you."

"It's a start."

Melody opened the card and took a deep breath, wondering if she could handle this. Her eyes blurred with mist as she read its tender message, then Matthew's arms came around her. "What's wrong, Melody?" he asked.

"I don't know," she admitted, pulling back. "I just feel all tied up in knots inside. It's like I'm standing on a bridge between the past and the future; or maybe it's between my family and the rest of my life."

"Or maybe it's both," he suggested.

She nodded. "And I feel so torn."

"Hey," Matthew urged her to a chair and sat down to face her, "I can't see inside your heart, Mel. I can't read your thoughts. But I think I know you well enough to know that you try very hard to do what's right. I know your Father in Heaven loves you very much, and you're entitled to a good life. Maybe I'm off base here, but if getting to the other side of that bridge is the right thing, wouldn't Satan be working very hard to keep you from getting there?"

Melody sniffled and looked into his eyes. She had to admit, "I never thought of it that way." He smiled, and she wondered once again how one man could bring so much love and wisdom into her life.

"Can we talk later?" he asked. "I'd like to take you out when you get off work."

"Okay," she said. "In the meantime, I better eat something and get back, or I'll never get off work."

Melody fixed her makeup again and they stopped at Taco Bell. As she was getting out of the car at the video store, Matthew said, "Oh, shoot. I left something at your apartment. Can I take your keys? I'll bring them back before you get off."

"Sure," she said, handing them over. "I'll see you later."

Through the afternoon, Melody contemplated what Matthew had said. It helped, but it didn't take away the turmoil. And she just didn't know what to do about it.

With Melody's keys in his possession, Matthew went back to his house to engage the second portion of his birthday plans. He'd talked to his parents about the idea, and they had gladly agreed to donate any amount of their old Christmas decorations that were no longer being used. Janna had made the comment that if Matthew married Melody, they would all stay in the family anyway.

Matthew's sisters were more than eager to help when they heard his plan, and he was grateful for their assistance. Time was short. He barely finished at Melody's apartment and took his sisters home before Melody got off work. When he walked into the store she glanced at her watch, saying, "I was beginning to think I'd have to walk home, since you have my car keys, too."

"Sorry," he said. "Time got away from me." On their way out to her car, he added, "I hope you know I wouldn't leave you stranded."

"Actually, I do. I wasn't worried."

Matthew smiled. "I'll follow you over, if that's okay. Then you can freshen up and we'll go as soon as you're ready."

"Sounds good to me," she said. As long as she was with Matthew, it was easier to avoid the discouragement that continued to hover around her.

Matthew followed close behind Melody as she drove. At one point he had to stop at a light while she went on ahead. He got nervous, fearing she'd arrive before he got there. But he pulled up in front of her apartment just as she was getting out of her car. As she approached the door, he took the keys from her hand and opened it for her.

Melody reached for the light switch as the door closed, but Matthew's hand was over it. In the moment it took her to question his motives, she realized that something was different. The twinkling, colored lights drew her attention and she turned abruptly. She teetered slightly and was grateful to feel Matthew's arms come around her from behind. She was too stunned to speak, too moved to respond.

"Happy birthday, Melody," Matthew whispered behind her ear.

Melody turned to look at him. Not knowing what to say, she scolded, "You told me you weren't going to spend any money to—"

"I told you I was going to give you a Christmas you'd never forget, and it had nothing to do with money. I didn't say I wouldn't *spend* any money. But this is for your birthday."

"But . . ." She turned and motioned toward the Christmas tree covered with twinkling lights and little decorations.

"I didn't spend a dime on decorations," he said. "It's all a bunch of leftovers from my mother's stash."

Melody didn't know what to say.

"You're not going to be mad at me, are you?" he asked. "I mean . . . it's kind of scary putting up a Christmas tree in somebody's house who hates Christmas. I was afraid you'd threaten to stuff it up my nose or something."

While Melody wasn't quite sure how to feel, she had to admit, "No, I'm not mad at you. It's beautiful. Thank you." She absorbed it again and sighed before she went into the other room to change her clothes and freshen up.

Matthew called his sisters from the kitchen phone, since they had been anxious to hear about Melody's reaction. When Melody came out of the bedroom, she said, "You didn't leave anything here today, did you."

"Yes, I did," he insisted. "I purposely left my wallet on the couch, so I could come back and get it."

"You're a rogue, Matthew Trevor," she laughed.

"Maybe I am."

"Shall we go?" she asked.

"Uh . . . not yet."

"What's wrong?"

"I think you've overlooked something."

Melody looked baffled as he pointed to the floor at the base of the tree. Only then did she notice a package sitting there, half hidden beneath its branches.

"Matthew!" she muttered. "You already gave me a present. You can't—"

Matthew kissed her to stop her protests. "Melody," he said, "I can't make up for twenty bad birthdays. But I'd like to try. Today has been one of the best days of my life. You cannot comprehend the joy it has given me to be able to do this for you. Please . . . just open it, and pretend you like it whether you do or not, okay?"

"I'll open it," she said, "but if I don't like it, you'll be the first to know."

"Okay," he smirked.

As Melody pulled out the large box, wrapped in red foil, she realized that this moment was something she had dreamed of often through her childhood. It didn't matter what was in the box. Matthew Trevor had already been the means to make her dreams come true.

Melody's hands were nearly shaking as she pulled off the ribbon and opened the box. She glanced skeptically at Matthew. He looked like a child watching a magic show. Melody took a deep breath and folded back the tissue, then she froze. In spite of what she had told him, the last thing she'd expected to find was this. She just stared at it, feeling like a penniless child looking through the window of a candy store. She couldn't bring herself to touch it.

Matthew finally said, "Aren't you going to try it on?"

She looked at him but still said nothing. Matthew pulled the long, black coat out of the box and held it up. It was double-breasted with simple lines; tailored, yet feminine. She hesitantly put her arms into the sleeves, closing her eyes to absorb the sensation, as if she was tasting chocolate for the first time.

"It's beautiful," she finally managed. "I can't believe it." She closed her eyes to absorb the feel of wearing a brandnew coat. It was something like the way she felt when Matthew Trevor kissed her. *Like the touch of an angel*. It was almost too good to be true.

Chapter Ten

"Shall we go, my lady?" he asked, holding out his arm for her. Melody smiled and allowed him to escort her to the car as if she was a queen.

Matthew took Melody to a fine restaurant. She gasped at the prices on the menu and insisted he take her elsewhere. He assured her that he could afford it—once in a while, at least. Once she got over the shock of the prices, she savored every bite, every aspect of the experience. Matthew just observed her, feeling as if he was seeing the world all over again through a child's eyes.

When they walked outside, she declared, "I've never been so full in my life. It was incredible."

"So, what now? It's your birthday. We'll do anything you want."

"I just want to be outside so I can wear this coat for the rest of my life."

Matthew chuckled. "Okay, we'll start with a walk."

Melody's thoughts wandered as they ambled up the street, neither of them prone to conversation. Christmas was thick in the air. Every house, every storefront—even the chill in the air—conveyed evidence that the holiday was nearly close enough to touch. While she was indulging in the reality that she had celebrated a birthday for the first time in her life, Melody hated the way her thoughts wandered elsewhere against her will. She wondered what her family was doing. But then, she didn't have to wonder. Her brothers were either out buying beer and cigarettes or sitting at home consuming them. Her mother was either lying around depressed, forcing herself to wash a few dishes, or cleaning up some mess or other left by her sons. Her sisters were groveling to dysfunctional men, which was likely the most repulsive thought of all. And none of them cared whether or not Christmas was here. Or maybe they did. She'd never bothered to ask any of them how they felt about their upbringing. She had just assumed the lifestyle didn't bother them because they'd always seemed comfortable with it. Or maybe they just didn't know any better. She had tried to show them a better life, given them opportunities for help and change, and it had gotten her nothing but more heartache. Why couldn't she just accept the reality that she could do nothing for them? Why couldn't she just let go and enjoy her own life?

"Where are you?" Matthew asked, nudging her gently.

"I don't know."

"You're lying."

"Okay, I don't want to talk about it."

"That's better." When she said nothing more, he guessed with a degree of certainty, "You're either thinking about your family, or you're dreading Christmas."

"Both," she answered, marveling at his perception. Or maybe she was just transparent.

"You know, Melody, I'm no expert, and maybe I'm way off base. But I think your biggest problem is simply that you believe you don't deserve to be happy when your family is miserable."

Melody stopped walking and looked up at him. The bright Christmas lights from a store window shone over his face.

"You've made choices, Melody. You've chosen to live the gospel and apply it in your life. You've chosen to avoid immorality and substance abuse. You have a right to be blessed for those choices."

"And my mother? What choices did she make, Matthew? She chose to marry a man, believing he would take care of her. From that moment, her choices were gone."

"She chose to stay with him."

"You think it's that easy?" she asked with cynicism.

Matthew looked at her hard. "No, Melody, it's not easy."

"How does a mother get away from something like that? How can she just—"

Matthew took hold of her shoulders and shook her gently. "I'll tell you how. She picks her battered body up off the floor. Then, with a prayer in her heart, she puts herself in God's hands and drags the suitcases up the stairs. She tries to explain to her son why he has to leave his room and his friends and most of his toys. And she cries while she struggles to put her whole life into a few pieces of luggage. Then she runs like hell and never looks back."

Melody absorbed his intensity and recalled what she'd almost forgotten. He knew what he was talking about from personal experience. "I'm sorry," she murmured, looking away.

Matthew touched her chin. "I'm not passing judgment on your mother, Melody. But every day of a person's life brings choices and consequences. Even doing nothing is a choice. And the fact is, you are not personally accountable for the choices of your family members."

"I know that," she cried. "In my heart, I know that, but . . . sometimes I just *ache,* and I don't understand why."

"Melody, you are an incredible woman. Don't expect to understand it all right now. Healing comes in layers. It may take the rest of your life to completely come to terms with it. But you're on the right path, and you're moving in the right direction. You're strong. You're faithful. And I love you."

Melody laughed to avoid sobbing. "Oh, Matthew. You're so good to me. Sometimes I guess I'm just . . . afraid I'll never overcome that Morgan mentality."

"And what is that?"

"Oh, it just seems they all believe that life gets no better. They believe it's circumstances, not choices, that make things the way they are. And even though I know that's not true, sometimes it's just hard. It's been in the family for generations. It's a difficult cycle to break."

"Yes, but you're breaking it. And I'm behind you every step of the way."

Melody looked up at him and smiled. How could she ever explain the way he touched her life?

"I have a suggestion," he said.

"For what?"

"For overcoming the Morgan mentality."

"And what is that?" she asked.

"You could change your name," he said, reaching into his coat pocket. He held a tiny box in front of her face. "How does Melody Noel Trevor sound?"

Matthew opened the box. Melody gasped as the ring appeared, reflecting the twinkling Christmas lights nearby. Earlier this evening, when Melody had put on her new coat, she had believed that nothing could be more wonderful. She was wrong. Like so many times before, she was speechless. Matthew had a way of doing that to her. She looked up into his eyes, somehow expecting to see some kind of doubt; something to justify her own concerns. But she saw nothing but raw sincerity. The love in his eyes was so apparent that she couldn't question it.

"I . . . I don't know what to say," she finally managed.

"Just say yes or no."

Finding the reality difficult to believe, she said, "What was the question . . . exactly? I seem to have missed that part."

Matthew laughed softly, then his voice deepened with sincerity. "Will you marry me?"

Inside Melody's head, the answer reverberated. *Yes! Yes! Yes!* But she couldn't force it to her lips. She was relieved when he broke the silence.

"I've fasted and prayed about this, Melody. I know in my heart that God wants us to be together. But I can't make that decision for you. You take all the time you need. And don't marry me unless you know beyond any doubt that it's right. Because that's what will get us through the rough times—knowing it was right."

"I need to think about it. It's all . . . so fast."

"I know. It's okay. I've got forever."

Melody glanced down at the ring again. "Can I try it on?"

"I was hoping you would."

Matthew slid the ring onto her finger and she sighed. "It is beautiful. You have good taste."

Matthew looked into her eyes. "Yes, I do."

"I meant in rings and coats."

"I meant in women."

Melody put the ring back in the box and closed it. "You just hold on to that. Maybe when I get past my pre-Christmas syndrome I'll be able to think more clearly."

"Okay." Matthew put the box back in his pocket. "Which reminds me . . . we haven't watched *Scrooge* yet."

Melody retorted lightly, "And I was having such a good day."

"Well, how about tomorrow, then?"

She looked at him as if to say, *Only if I have to*. Matthew laughed and wrapped her hand around his arm as they walked on.

When Matthew took Melody back to her apartment, it was almost as difficult to say good night as it was to take off her coat. After he left, she sat for a long while in the little front room with only the Christmas tree lights on. They gave the room a magical atmosphere, and she could almost feel Matthew's love surrounding her, even in his absence.

Melody finally turned off the tree lights and went to bed, but it was long after that when she finally slept. She had a choice before her. It wasn't something vague and obscure anymore. Matthew Trevor had asked her to marry him. She pondered what the reality of that might be like. There was no question that he would be a blessing to her life, but she wondered what influence she might have on *his* life. Could she overcome the dysfunction of her child-hood to be a good wife and mother? Of course, if she said no, they would have to go their separate ways eventually. And that was a thought she couldn't bear. Still, the fear of losing him was not enough to base such a decision on. She had to consider what was best for both of them in the long run.

Melody finally slept with the resolve to fast and pray, as he had challenged her. She went to work without break-fast and skipped lunch, keeping a prayer in her heart throughout the day. Late in the afternoon, she had a strong impression that she should call Matthew's mother. She tried to talk herself out of it, but the feeling was too strong to ignore. Finally she called, relieved that Matthew didn't answer the phone. "Hi, this is Melody," she said, wishing she wasn't so nervous.

"Hello, Melody. Matthew's at work, but I can—"

"No, actually . . . I was wondering if I could talk to *you*. I know how busy you are, but . . ."

"Oh, I'd be happy to."

"I'll be off work in less than an hour, but I'll work around your schedule. If today's not good for you, then . . ."

Janna graciously offered to meet Melody at her apartment as soon as the family had eaten; then they could talk without interruptions. When Janna arrived, Melody felt more nervous than she'd anticipated. "I hope it wasn't a problem to get away from your family."

"Oh, don't you worry about it," Janna insisted. "They can fend for themselves well enough. I'm glad you called. I've been wanting to get to know you a little better—one on one. And truthfully, I needed to get out of the house. It was good timing."

Melody offered Janna a seat in the front room, trying to find a place to start this conversation. She sat down across from Janna just as she asked, "So, what's on your mind?"

Melody had to admit to something she'd thought all along. "You seem too young to be Matthew's mother."

Janna chuckled. "I was very young when he was born. It's just difficult for me to believe how quickly he's grown."

Melody looked down at her hands and got to the point. "He asked me to marry him."

"Yes, I know."

"The two of you are very close."

"Well," Janna said, "I don't think he tells me *everything,* but yes, I'd say we're close."

"I don't know how much he's told you about my background; my family. Not that I would mind if he told you. It would save me from having to tell you."

"He's told me a little. We talked about it the day he met your mother. I think he told you why that was difficult for him. It brought up some things we'd rather keep in the past."

"I must say it's difficult for me to believe—that you've survived something so horrible, I mean. In some ways, your first husband sounds worse than my father, which is hard for me to imagine." Knowing that Matthew's feelings toward his stepfather were so intense, Melody felt compelled to ask, "Whatever happened to him? Have you seen him since . . ." She didn't know how to put it without sounding insensitive.

"That last time we saw him," Janna said, "he'd gotten out of prison on parole—for the third time, mind you—and he broke into the house. Dustin was a baby, and Matthew was getting ready to send in his mission papers. Russell pulled a gun on me. Matthew saved me that day, but I realized then that his feelings toward his stepfather were deep and raw. I think he's come far with those feelings; even the experience he had the day he met your mother has taken his healing a step further. I'm certain he'll be fine."

"Where is he now . . . your ex-husband?"

Janna sighed. "He was sent back to prison for life, since he'd blown it one too many times. Word came a while back that he had killed himself. I'm ashamed to say that the thought gave me a great deal of peace."

Melody chuckled with no humor. "Should I be ashamed to say, then, that I felt no grief or remorse when my father died? Because I didn't, and I still don't."

Melody felt Janna looking intently at her, as if something intangible connected between them. "It would seem that you and I understand each other," Janna said.

"Perhaps we do," Melody admitted, "but . . . I look at you and see so much strength. And inside I feel so . . . well, it's difficult to explain. I guess that's what I wanted to talk to you about—at least part of it. Matthew told me what you went through with your first husband. I must say I was surprised. To see you now . . . it's difficult to believe. I don't want to put you on the spot or anything, but I just have to ask: how did you do it? How did you rise above it to become so strong? So confident?"

Janna laughed softly. "Well, don't go assuming that my life is completely free of struggle. It's certainly not. But we have come a long way. And I've learned a great deal since the days when I allowed my circumstances to rule me."

Janna sighed, looking even deeper into Melody's eyes, as if she could somehow see into her soul. "You haven't told me exactly what you're concerned about right now, Melody, but I think I could guess. So, let me just tell you some of the things I learned that made a difference. Maybe it will help."

Melody leaned forward eagerly as Janna Trevor shared a brief summary of her life's struggles. She had been a sexual abuse victim, who had later found herself unwed and pregnant. And then she had married a violent man. But even after getting away from her horrible first marriage, the effects of the abuse lingered with her.

"I went through extensive counseling—more than once. I drove Colin away for a time. I had an emotional breakdown after the girls were born. For a while, I wasn't even capable of caring for my children. The details aren't important, Melody; what I learned is. When I was finally able to put the pieces together, there were a few points that made a difference. I learned that life happens *from* me, not *to* me." She allowed Melody a moment to absorb her statement before she went on. "Which, in essence, means that no matter what life dishes out to me, I have the ability to respond to it with wisdom, maturity, and dignity. I *am* in control of my circumstances. It's as simple as that."

Janna sighed and lifted one leg up beneath her. She seemed as comfortable as if they were college roommates. "Going along with that," she continued, "I learned that my Father in Heaven loved me, and he wanted me to be happy. As I learned to rely on the Lord, he led me to the people and information I needed to solve my problems and keep me going.

"I look back now and realize that most of my agony could have been avoided if I had accepted one thing." Janna leaned forward and looked directly into Melody's eyes. "God sent a man into my life who was willing to love me in spite of anything from my past. And because I wasn't willing to believe in that love, I pushed him away—more than once, and I created a great deal of heartache for all of us."

Janna took hold of Melody's hand. "I can't make your decisions for you, Melody. I don't know your heart. But if I can share something with you that will help save you some of the same grief, then by all means, I will. What you do with it is up to you. I don't know what your relationship with Matthew is like beyond what I see, and what he tells me. I'd like to think I know my son well, and truthfully, he is so much like his father. But, Melody, if I could go back and do it over, there is one thing I would have done differently. For that reason, I want you to think about this. If

God sends you a knight on a white horse, just jump in the saddle with him and hold on. Because if you stand there trying to convince him that he shouldn't rescue you—that you don't deserve his love—you could both get devoured by dragons."

Melody pondered the advice for a minute, marveling at Janna's insight and how the things she had said applied to her own circumstances. But she still had to admit, "Sometimes I wonder if I have what it takes to make him happy; if I can overcome my past enough to—"

"That is exactly what I'm talking about," Janna interrupted. "I cannot count the times I asked myself that very thing. Colin only wanted to love me and take care of me, and I just couldn't accept it. It took an emotional breakdown and a separation to force me to my senses."

"But what if problems come up that—"

"Melody, I want to tell you one thing about Matthew, and then I really think you have all the information you need to make a decision." Janna lifted a finger, and her eyes became intense. "Matthew fully understands the true depth of commitment in the face of the worst kind of problems. The other night, he came to Colin and me and asked us, 'What would you say if I told you I was going to marry a woman with a dysfunctional upbringing?' And do you know what Colin told him? He said, 'Love her unconditionally. Love her enough to let her solve her own problems. And don't ever, ever give up on her.'"

Janna took a deep breath, and Melody sensed that there was some part of this story that she didn't understand. She wanted to ask, but felt it was inappropriate.

Janna finished by saying, "That means a lot coming from a man who has been put through hell because his wife was an abuse victim. Colin's had his struggles, but he's a good man and he loves me. Eventually he taught me that life is good and full and meant to be enjoyed. But Melody, you are so much stronger than I was when I married Colin. Matthew told me how you handled your sister, and your attitude about your family. I know it's hard, but it's the best thing."

"Sometimes I wonder."

"Don't wonder. Just listen to the Spirit and build your own life. I filed a restraining order against my father. And I haven't seen him since, thank heaven."

Melody took a deep breath, as if she could literally breathe in Janna Trevor's example and experience. And she couldn't deny the peace she felt. In that moment, she almost believed she *could* be happy—in spite of anything that might have happened in her past. And at the same time, she knew in her heart that she would be a fool to turn down the prospect of eternity with a man like Matthew Trevor. He loved her, and he'd made it repeatedly clear that he was committed to her. And, perhaps equally important, she knew in her heart that it was the right thing to do. There was an undeniable warmth inside that seemed to confirm Janna's words. *If God sends you a knight on a white horse, just jump in the saddle with him and hold on.* In that moment she recalled how perfectly secure she felt when Matthew's arms were around her.

"I can only guess what you're thinking," Janna said, startling Melody from her thoughts. "But from that serene little smile on your face, I have to assume it's good."

Melody laughed softly, blushing at the thought of having her mind read. She was tempted to share her thoughts, but they still felt so new and fragile. She needed time to mull it all around and be absolutely certain before she told *anyone*.

"I feel much better," Melody said, impulsively hugging Janna tightly. "I can't tell you how much you've helped me."

"I'm glad I could. And I want you to know, Melody, whether things work out with you and Matthew or not, you are still welcome in our home anytime."

Melody pulled back and nodded, too moved to speak.

"Your tree is beautiful," Janna commented, nodding toward the Christmas tree Matthew had given her.

"I guess you know how it got here," Melody smiled.

"Matthew always loved Christmas—much like his father. I mean, I grew up celebrating Christmas, but it was just my mother and me, and she was more passive about it. But Colin *loved* Christmas. His family made a big deal of it. The first Christmas I spent with him and Matthew was like a dream. Now I can't imagine doing it any other way."

Again Melody sighed deeply, contemplating how much Matthew had touched her life already in that respect. She wondered if any woman had ever been so blessed.

Chapter Eleven

Janna was about to leave Melody's apartment when the phone rang. "You haven't seen my mother, have you?" Matthew asked.

"And what if I have?" Melody answered.

"Dad said she was with you."

"Yes," Melody drawled, wanting to make him sweat.

"And?"

"And what? We've been talking."

Janna smiled as it became obvious who Melody was talking to.

"About what?" Matthew asked.

"A lot of things. Do you want to talk to her?"

"I can do that later. The kids were just talking about watching *Scrooge* tonight. Dad said they could, since there's no school tomorrow. Do you want to come over and—"

"I'd love to." She put her hand over the mouthpiece to say to Janna, "He says they're going to watch *Scrooge*."

"Well, let's go," Janna said, coming to her feet. "You can ride over with me, and Matthew can bring you back."

"We'll see you in a few minutes," Melody said to Matthew and hung up the phone.

Melody didn't know if it was a softening of her attitude that made the movie so impressive, or if it was just a phenomenal movie. Maybe a little of both. At one point while the video was paused for Dustin to take a bathroom break, Matthew told Melody the story of Dickens' circumstances when he wrote the book. The story was undoubtedly inspired, and it literally saved Dickens from sinking into poverty. Matthew also told her that he had seen many versions of *A Christmas Carol* on film, but this particular one, a musical version made in England, was by far his favorite. He pointed out how the music had a way of speaking to one's spirit. As the movie progressed, Melody understood what he meant. She cried through the entire last half of the movie, while Matthew just held her hand and kept her supplied with tissues.

It was nearly midnight when Matthew drove Melody home. In the car he said, "You're awfully quiet."

Melody wondered how to explain the feelings going on inside of her.

"I assume you liked the movie."

"It was incredible," she admitted.

"Is something bothering you?" he asked.

"Yes, but . . ." She struggled for the words to explain. "Have you ever just . . . felt something that you couldn't quite explain? And it's like there's this mist between what you feel and being able to understand it."

"That's exactly how I felt after you took me to your mother's house."

Melody's feelings intensified as she recalled what he had experienced that day. By the time Matthew pulled the car up in front of her apartment, she was beginning to have a glimmer of understanding. And it scared her. She was wondering how to ask Matthew if he would stay a while when he asked, "Are you okay?"

"I don't think so. Will you come in with me?"

Matthew nodded and got out to open her door. When they were sitting on the floor, with only the Christmas tree lights on, Matthew said, "I get the feeling the movie left an impression on you. Is that why you're—"

"I don't know, but . . ." Her eyes became distant, and Matthew knew somehow that she was encountering some difficult memories. "I think . . . the reason Christmas has always been so difficult for me is . . . well, I believe there were times in my childhood when I . . . caught a glimpse of the spirit of Christmas. But . . . one day I just . . . had to shut it down."

The memories suddenly became clear, and Melody wanted only to push them away. Her chest tightened and a hard knot formed in her stomach. She groaned and squeezed her eyes shut, forgetting that she wasn't alone until Matthew's arms came around her. She heard him speak but couldn't discern his words; only that they were gentle and soothing. And the protection of his embrace made anything bearable.

Melody lost all sense of time as she cried in Matthew's arms, while unwanted memories filed through her mind like a regiment of Nazi soldiers marching through an otherwise peaceful village. Their threat was ominous and frightening. And her only peace was in the belief that they would march right through and leave her in peace.

When Melody's emotion ran down, she found herself curled up on the floor, her head in Matthew's lap, staring at the twinkling Christmas lights that illuminated the room with a soft glow.

"Tell me, Melody." Matthew's gentle voice broke the silence. "Give me your memories and I'll throw them away—once and for all." Melody closed her eyes and could almost imagine her angel hero sitting where Matthew sat now. But his features were no longer obscure. It was easy to imagine Matthew Trevor dressed in Nephite armor, ready to ward off the demons that plagued her. He was her protector, her rescuer. And it was easy for her to talk to him about things she'd once believed she could never say aloud.

"My father was a horrible man, Matthew. I remember soon after he died, I tried for days to think of a fond memory, of some indication of warmth. But there was nothing. I honestly cannot remember one good thing about my father."

Melody sighed, briefly taking note of the way Matthew combed his fingers through her hair. "As a young child, I probably just assumed that life in my home was normal; that all children lived in fear of their fathers, and never had anything good to make life worth living. When I started going to school, I began to realize how different we were. But nothing made that so evident as the coming of Christmas. I'll never forget how I raised my hand in kindergarten and asked the teacher what Christmas was. The other children laughed, and I was so embarrassed. After that, I just pretended I knew what was going on, even when I didn't. I loved all the Christmas activities at school, and I tried to be involved, but . . ."

Matthew could tell they were getting to a sensitive point by the way her voice faltered. "I think it was third grade, and the class was doing a gift exchange. The teacher said we didn't have to buy a gift. We could bring something from home, or make something. I was so excited to think that if I brought a gift for another child in the class, I could actually come home with my very own Christmas gift. I talked to my mother about it, and since I had a little money saved, she was going to take me to town to get something. But . . ." Melody's tears returned. Her words were strained. "He . . . was so . . . drunk that night. He . . . raged . . . and screamed. He . . . called Christmas nothing more than an excuse for robbing a man of hard-earned cash. He took my money . . . away and . . . told me he would . . . put it to better use. He . . . slapped me hard, and . . . he told me if I . . . if I . . ." Melody cried cleansing tears as it all suddenly made sense.

Matthew wondered if she would get past her emotion enough to finish the statement. But she sat up abruptly, looking into his eyes as she spoke with vehemence. "He told me if I ever said the word Christmas again, he'd give me a beating I'd never forget. That's it, Matthew," she cried. "That's why it's been so hard for me. He outlawed Christmas; banished it from our lives, and he reinforced it with corporal punishment. I didn't go to school the day they exchanged gifts. And every year after that, I just stayed in the background while the Christmas activities were taking place. If they were doing something I couldn't handle, I just wouldn't go. I just . . . stopped . . . *feeling* Christmas, because . . . it was the only way I could . . . survive."

"Oh, Melody," Matthew murmured, pressing a hand to her face. Then he pulled her into his arms, wishing he could somehow ease the pain. "I can't change the past, Melody, and I can't take away the hurt of what he did to you. But he's gone now. And I will do everything in my power to make your future bright and good. I *swear* it."

Melody cried herself to sleep in Matthew's arms. Her next awareness was the sensation of being lifted. It took her a moment to realize that Matthew was carrying her to her bed. He pulled off her shoes and tucked her in, pressing a kiss to her brow.

"I love you, Matthew," she said.

"I love you, too, Melody." He touched her face. "Are you going to be all right?"

Melody nodded. "I think I feel better."

"Good," he said. "Sometimes you just have to take those things out and look at them. And once you do, it doesn't seem quite so bad . . . because you know you can get beyond it."

"I guess you would know."

Matthew nodded. He kissed her brow again, then told her good night. All the way home he wished he could have stayed with her, just to be close to her. But he shed a few tears on her behalf then went to sleep in his own bed, praying with everything he had that she would want to share her future with him. *He loved her so much.*

After Matthew left, Melody couldn't go back to sleep. As she contemplated the healing that had taken place inside her during the last several hours, her mind raced with her heart. Putting this experience together with all she had learned since Matthew Trevor had come into her life, she thought and felt things she'd never considered before. She was drawn to the book *A Christmas Carol* that Matthew had given her weeks ago. And once she started to read, she couldn't put it down. Dickens could be difficult to follow at times, but having seen the movie, she was able to clearly imagine the scenes he described. And just as when she read the scriptures with an open heart, Melody could see the symbolism in the story, and she was able to grasp the deeper messages.

Melody read until four in the morning, then she cried herself to sleep, grateful that she had the day off work. She woke up late in the morning, physically drained but spiritually filled. She lay in bed for a long while, feeling as if she'd just emerged from a dream. It was a beautiful, wonderful dream, where love was real and the spirit of Christmas surrounded her in abundance.

Finally she reached for the phone and dialed the store where Matthew worked. When he came to the phone, she asked, "When do you get off?"

"In about forty-five minutes. Why?"

"Well, why don't you come and get me? Unless you've got something better to do, of course."

"I'll see you in an hour," he said, then he broke into that delighted little laugh he was famous for.

Melody hurried to shower and make her bed. She was eating a piece of toast when she heard him pull up. She grabbed her coat as she opened the door. Then she gasped. "It's snowing!"

Matthew turned his flake-covered head to look behind him, as if he'd just now noticed that the world was blanketed in white. "It appears that way," he said. Then he laughed. She was obviously feeling better. "Where have you been?"

"In bed, actually," she admitted. He helped her into her coat and she stepped outside. "Oh, my gosh! It's so beautiful."

Matthew laughed as she spread her arms and lifted her face heavenward, letting the huge flakes caress her skin.

"I thought you hated snow, Melody Noel," he said.

Melody smiled at Matthew, feeling as if her heart would burst. She couldn't hold back the tears as she said, "But this is Christmas snow, Matthew. We're going to have a white Christmas."

Matthew was stunned. From that first time she'd made her declarations of hating Christmas, he'd wanted more than anything to convince her otherwise. But he'd known all along that her discovery of the spirit of Christmas had to come from within. And he'd truly wondered if it would happen. *But it had!*

While he was wondering what to say, Melody wrapped her arms around his neck and pressed her mouth over his. "I love you," she whispered, then she lifted her face skyward again and laughed. In the midst of her laughter, Matthew picked her up, twirled her around, then laid her down in the snow.

"What are you doing?" she squealed.

"Haven't you ever made snow angels?" he asked.

"Not since I was four," she replied, then she laughed again as she and Matthew lay side by side, moving their arms and legs back and forth, then standing carefully to see the images of angels left in the snow.

"Angels are wonderful things, you know," Melody said.

"What kind of angels?" Matthew asked, watching her face closely.

"Oh, all kinds." She looked skyward again, as if she could see them in the heavily falling snow. "There are the angels who told the shepherds that Christ was born. And the angel in his tomb who said that he had risen." She closed her eyes and sighed. "There are angels who take little lost children to Primary. And there are angels who stand guard over frightened little girls, like great Nephite warriors. Some angels work on the other side of the veil, and some work in the flesh, here in this world, living their lives in a way that allows them to be instruments in God's hands." She looked into Matthew's eyes and touched his face. "Then there are angels who appear out of nowhere on figurative white horses, who spread the spirit of Christmas like frosting on a star-shaped cookie. They rescue women who spill their purses and have no money for bus fare." She kissed him quickly and added, "You're my hero angel, Matthew. And I want to be with you forever."

Matthew felt his eyes widen. His heart began to pound. What was she saying? Before he had a chance to ask, she reached down to grab a handful of snow and pressed it into his face. Then she ran. She ran like a child, her long black coat billowing out behind her, her laughter intruding delightfully on the silence of the falling snow. Matthew took a moment to absorb the picture she created before he ran after her. She giggled like a little girl as he grabbed her and rolled into the snow, bringing her with him.

Melody squealed with laughter, attempting to break free until she found herself lying on her back, looking up into his face. He pressed her arms to the ground, leaving her helpless. But it was the look in his eyes that stopped her laughter. She was wondering if she'd done something wrong when he spoke in a gravelly voice. "I'd swear I just heard you say that you want to be with me forever. But then, I'm also getting the impression that you rather like snow, and you might actually be anticipating Christmas. Is the real you finally emerging? Or are you just experiencing some kind of brief hysteria?"

"I don't know what it is, Matthew," she said, oblivious to the cold ground beneath her. "I only know that I want to feel this way for the rest of eternity. I want to spend every Christmas for the rest of my life dancing in the snow, and making funny little cookies, and decorating trees, and putting lights on rooftops. And I want to do it with you. I want to marry you, Matthew Trevor, and I know in my heart that no matter what we might come up against, we'll make it . . . because we'll be together."

Melody wasn't prepared for the tears that rose in Matthew's eyes. He hugged her tightly and rolled onto his back, bringing her with him. While Melody was looking down at him, he said, "Do I detect a change of heart?"

Melody arched her head back and laughed, then she nuzzled her face against Matthew's throat, saying softly, "I read *A Christmas Carol* last night. I finished it sometime early this morning, and I cried myself to sleep. When I woke up, I realized that I had learned something I never expected."

"Tell me," he urged.

"I learned that the spirit of Christmas is something so much bigger and deeper than I ever comprehended. And the true angels in this world are the ones who keep that spirit in their hearts all year round. I want to be that kind of person, Matthew. I want to make a difference in this world, the way a few select people have made a difference for me. And I believe in my heart that with you as my ally, I can be anything."

Matthew touched her face and looked into her eyes. "Should I take that as a yes?"

Melody positively smirked. "What was the question again, exactly?"

"Will you marry me, Melody Noel?"

"Only if it's forever."

Matthew laughed and rolled her into the snow again. They finally yielded to the cold and went into the apartment, where they spread their coats over the kitchen chairs and Melody heated water for hot chocolate. She was digging in the cupboard for marshmallows when Matthew took hold of her left hand. She caught her breath as he slid the ring onto her third finger. She sighed, then pushed her arms around his shoulders, holding him tightly.

Matthew returned her embrace, feeling as if he'd been born for this moment. He'd never been happier in his life.

While they were sharing hot chocolate, Melody's mind began to wander. "Matthew," she said, "I wish that . . ." She hesitated, almost afraid to say it out loud. It seemed so preposterous.

"What do you wish?" he asked.

"Well . . . I feel it . . . I guess it's the spirit of Christmas. Or maybe it's just an aspect of feeling the Holy Ghost that I've never experienced before. But . . . I wish I could share it . . . with my family." She sighed. "Actually, let me be more specific. I think Lisa and my brothers are past hope. That's sad, I know; but I can honestly say I don't remember ever seeing anything redeemable in them. Maybe in the next life they'll have a chance to see things differently. On the other hand, I've always had hopes for Lydia. I always felt like there was something in her that could be reached. Unfortunately, even though I've tried, there's nothing more I can do for her right now. But . . . I wish my mother could feel this way, Matthew." She pressed a fist to her heart. "I wish there was something I could give her . . . some kind of Christmas gift . . . that might offer a glimpse of what life could really be like."

"I don't think that sounds so impossible. We've still got some shopping time left." He glanced at his watch. "A little, anyway."

"Okay," Melody leaned back and folded her arms, "but . . . I don't know what I'd get her. I mean . . . a toaster or a blender isn't really going to have a lot of impact. I don't know if there's anything I can give her that won't just become somehow . . . absorbed into that awful house. I need to give her something that her children can't take away from her or defile."

"Okay, like what?" Matthew asked.

Melody sighed. "I have no idea."

A few minutes later she asked, "So, what are we doing for Christmas anyway?" Her voice picked up a facetious lilt. "Do your plans include your fiancée?"

"Absolutely!" He grinned. "I was hoping you'd just want to spend Christmas with my family." He leaned toward her, lifting his brows comically, "You know, Mel, there are advantages to the situation with your family."

"How do you figure?" she asked skeptically.

"We'll never have to argue about which family to spend holidays with."

Melody smiled. "No contest there."

"Well, since tomorrow is Christmas Eve, I was hoping you could come and spend the day. We'll be doing all kinds of things to get ready. And my mother told me to ask you if you want to spend the night. We have a spare room. We're busy pretty late Christmas Eve, and the fun starts early the next morning." He grinned again. "She said she didn't want you to miss anything. What do you think?"

"If you're sure it's all right, I guess—"

"All right? My mother was practically gushing over the idea. She adores you."

Melody attempted to absorb that along with every-thing else. Life just kept getting better every minute.

"Okay," she said, "so what do I need? I mean, is this a formal occasion, or what? I've never done Christmas before."

"It's all very casual . . . except for Christmas dinner. You might want to bring a dress for that."

Melody tried to imagine herself as part of some grand Christmas feast, and a thought occurred to her. "If we're spending the next two days with your family, I think we should go shopping—right now."

"Did you think of something to get your mother?"

"No, but I'm going to buy myself a new dress. I have *never* bought myself a new dress. But I have some money put away, and I think this is an occasion that calls for something new."

"What an excellent idea." Matthew stood and held out his hand.

"And with any luck, you'll come up with something to get my mother."

"Me?" he protested, helping her into her coat.

"Well, you're the Christmas king."

Matthew laughed and walked her out to the car. It was still snowing, though not nearly as hard as it had been earlier. When they arrived at the mall, Melody commented, "I've got to be out of my mind. What kind of idiot goes to a mall on December twenty-third?"

"I do," Matthew said. "Are you calling me an idiot?"

"Only if you're the idiot who's going to marry me."

"Guilty," he said. Then he laughed and kissed her hand as they trudged across the crowded parking lot.

After getting a quick bite to eat, Melody led the way into ZCMI where she perused the racks of nice dresses, occasionally handing one to Matthew. When he had several, she took them into a dressing room to try them on. "You wait right there," she said over her shoulder. "I'll need your opinion."

"Yes, my lady," he said, and she laughed.

The first three dresses Melody tried on provoked the same response in Matthew. "It's nice," he said. "Whatever you think."

At the fourth dress, he said, "I really don't like that." And the fifth inspired the response, "That is horrible!"

"Well, at least I know you have an opinion," she said, going back in to try on the last one she'd picked out.

Melody barely glanced at herself in the mirror before she stepped out of the dressing room. But she knew this was the right dress when Matthew's eyes brightened. She turned in front of the three-way mirror to get the full effect. The red shimmery fabric was fitted over the bodice, then flared out at the waist, hanging to mid-calf. It had simple lines that only enhanced its elegance. "What do you think?" she asked.

"Whatever that dress costs, it's worth every penny."

"I guess you like it."

"That dress makes you look . . . like Christmas. That's it, Melody Noel—you look like Christmas."

Melody looked at herself again in the mirror, marveling at the changes in her life. Then, just as every time she considered how blessed she was, she couldn't help thinking of her family—her mother, specifically. And her heart ached.

"You know," she said to Matthew, "I remember my mother looking through the Sears catalog. I don't know if she *ever* ordered anything. But she'd look for hours at the dresses, and many times she'd say something like, 'Isn't that a beautiful color? Oh, to have a new dress and someplace to wear it.'"

As soon as Melody said it, she turned to look at Matthew. His expression told her he'd had the same idea. "A dress," they both said at the same time, then they laughed.

Melody put her own clothes back on and had Matthew hold the dress she'd picked out for herself while she perused the racks again, searching for the perfect dress for her mother. "Blue," she said. "It has to be blue." Then she prayed inwardly for help in finding the right dress. It occurred to her that these dresses were designed for younger women, so she led Matthew to a different section of the store. And within minutes, Melody found the perfect dress. She knew exactly what size to get, and when the two dresses were rung up at the cash register, Melody gasped to realize they had both been on sale, with an extra twenty percent off. "I saved so much money," she said to Matthew, "I can afford to get us both new shoes."

Matthew laughed and allowed her to lead him through several shoe stores before she found what she wanted.

"Okay," she said as they left the mall, "she'll have the dress, but she needs someplace to go. We need to get her out of that house and take her somewhere really special. Got any ideas?"

"How about Christmas dinner with my family?" Matthew suggested.

Melody didn't know if that was a good idea or not. "Maybe you should ask your mother before you—"

"I'll ask her, but I know she'd be delighted."

Melody thought about it a minute. She wasn't concerned about her mother behaving inappropriately. If they could get Thelma away from her dysfunctional children, even for a few hours, maybe it would be good for all of them.

"Okay, we'll talk to your mom, but . . . is there something we could give my mother . . . like . . . I know! I know! Tickets. Tickets to something . . . a play or something. We could take her and she could wear her dress, and—"

"The Nutcracker," Matthew said.

"What's that?"

Matthew laughed. "Oh, you are amazing! The Nutcracker, Melody. It's a Christmas ballet."

"A ballet?"

"Yeah. Our family goes every year between Christmas and New Year's Day. It's wonderful. You'd love it, and so would your mother. But . . ."

"But what?"

"Tickets can be hard to get this late. My mother would already have them for our family, but we can try. Before we see the Nutcracker, we always go out to eat, and then to Temple Square to see the Christmas lights."

"Oh, that would be perfect!" Melody exclaimed, praying in her heart that there might be a way to get tickets to the Nutcracker—whatever it was.

"Hey," he said, "before we go home, can I take you to meet somebody?"

"Sure, I guess," she said, wondering if she ought to be nervous. "Who?"

"Just friends of the family. They don't live far from here." He grinned. "I told them about you on the phone. They said if we got engaged, they wanted to be some of the first to know."

"Okay," she said, but she still felt nervous.

Matthew drove the car into a neighborhood of newer, beautiful homes and parked the car in a particular driveway. Melody took a deep breath as he rang the doorbell. A woman answered the door who looked older than Matthew, but younger than his mother.

"Matthew!" she squealed and hugged him. "Come in. It's freezing out there. Oh, my gosh. This must be Melody."

"It sure is," Matthew said proudly as they stepped inside and the door was closed.

"Your mom keeps telling me how wonderful this girl is. I wondered when we'd get to meet her."

"Well, here she is," Matthew announced. "Melody, I'd like you to meet Hilary Hayden, my mother's best friend for many years. Hilary, this is Melody . . . soon to be Trevor."

"Are you serious?" Hilary laughed and hugged Melody. "Your mom didn't tell me it was official."

"Well, it wasn't until today. Actually," Matthew said, "Mom doesn't know yet. So pretend you haven't heard."

"No problem," Hilary said. "Sit down. Are you hungry? I've got dinner cooking."

"Oh, that's okay," Matthew said. "We can't stay, but—"

"Well, Jack's in bathing Erin. You can't leave yet."

"We're not in *that* big of a hurry," Matthew said. Then he pointed to the Christmas tree. "You always have such a nice tree. I love it."

"Oh, Jack puts a great deal of effort into it. Personally, I think he gets some of his Christmas convictions from spending so much time in your home. Not that I'm complaining."

"I can relate to that," Melody said, realizing that she liked this Hilary. She also noticed that Matthew was extremely comfortable here.

A little girl, somewhere between two and three, ran into the front room. She was wrapped in a huge towel, her hair dripping.

"Erin," Hilary said, "go tell Daddy to get your clothes." She ignored her mother and stopped to survey their visitors. "Look who's here," Hilary said to her daughter. "It's Uncle Matthew. I bet he's got tickle bugs hiding in his pockets."

"Hey there, baby girl," Matthew said, then he wiggled his fingers inside his shirt pocket. Erin squealed and giggled as she ran down the hall. She came back a minute later wearing only her underwear. Melody heard a man's voice from the hallway. "Erin, you little beast." Then he laughed just before he appeared. Melody fought to keep her expression steady when she realized that Hilary's husband was in a wheelchair.

"Hey, Matthew," he said, grabbing little Erin with one arm to set her on his lap, where he efficiently helped her into an undershirt and nightgown. "What is this? You finally bring a girl to meet us?"

"They're engaged, Jack," Hilary said with enthusiasm.

"That's great," Jack laughed and set Erin free after he hugged her tightly. Then to his wife, "We did that two or three times, didn't we?"

"Something like that," Hilary said warmly.

"Well, introduce me," Jack said, moving toward Melody and extending a hand.

"Melody, this is Jack Hayden. He's something close to a big brother to me. Jack, this is Melody."

"It's a pleasure, Melody. We've heard nothing but good about you."

"The pleasure is mine," Melody said eagerly, loving the warmth she felt in this home. She was intrigued by Jack and Hilary, and wondered about their history.

"How's the judge?" Jack asked. "I haven't seen him for a while."

"He's the same as ever. Christmastime keeps him busy."

"Ah yes," Jack laughed, "he's well known for that. And your mother?"

"Fine. Everyone's fine. How are you doing?"

"Great. Life just keeps getting better." He smiled at his wife. "Hilary's pregnant. We're excited about that."

"And a little nervous," Hilary added. "After the way I had to stay down the last time, I know it's not going to be easy. But it will be worth it."

Melody noticed the look Jack gave his wife; it was much the way Matthew looked at her. She felt warm inside to know that she understood how it felt to be looked at that way.

Hilary ended up talking Matthew and Melody into staying for dinner. By the time they left, Melody felt as if she'd known them forever.

"Hey," Jack said when they were leaving, "when you get settled and get done with school, let me know. We'll get you a good deal on a home."

"Thanks," Matthew said, hugging Melody after he helped her into her coat. "We'll look forward to it." Matthew explained to Melody, "Jack is co-owner of a construction company that specializes in building homes. They built this whole neighborhood, didn't they?"

"Just about," Jack said.

"It was so good to meet you," Hilary said, hugging Matthew, then Melody. She added to Melody, "That is a beautiful coat."

"Thank you. Matthew gave it to me for my birthday."

"Good taste," Jack said, "in coats—and women."

"I'll agree with that," Matthew said.

In the car, Melody said, "Wow. That was incredible."

"What do you mean?" Matthew asked as they drove away.

"They're just wonderful people."

"Yes, they are."

"What did Jack mean when he said they'd been engaged two or three times?"

"Oh, they were engaged when the accident happened, and the wedding had to be postponed several months."

"The accident?"

"That paralyzed him."

"They were *engaged?*"

"That's right. When Jack got out of the hospital, he stayed with us until they were able to get married."

"Wow," Hilary said again. "Being with them is . . . inspiring."

"Yes, it is," Matthew agreed. "If I ever get feeling sorry for myself, all I have to do is think of Jack."

"Okay," Melody said, "at the risk of embarrassing myself, I have to know. That child is the spitting image of Jack. And they said Hilary's pregnant again. But I thought . . ."

"Erin really is his natural daughter," Matthew said. "They make a nice family, don't they?"

"They sure do. It's amazing how much he does; how well he gets around."

"Oh, that's not the half of it. That man has been camping with the young men. In fact, he served as Young Men's president for years. His independence and positive attitude are amazing—especially considering the fact that he had a pretty shaky upbringing."

"He did?"

"His mother was an alcoholic, for one thing."

Melody sighed and said it again. "Wow." For several minutes she just tried to absorb the impression these people had left on her—the hope it gave her in regard to her own future and conquering her own Goliaths. She was glad Matthew had taken her to meet them, and grateful for the events of this day. She'd never been so happy, or felt so much hope, in her entire life.

That night, Melody could hardly sleep. But her mind wasn't smoldering with confusion and guilt as it often had been before now. She was so excited about the next two days that she could hardly bear it. Tomorrow was Christmas Eve, and she was going to enjoy every minute.

The following morning, while she was packing an overnight bag, Melody realized that she had no Christmas gift for Matthew. "How could I be so stupid?" she scolded herself aloud. Of course, she'd never bought Christmas gifts before. But she had to get him *something*. He was her fiancé, for heaven's sake.

Melody called Matthew and told him she had to take care of something. "So don't come and get me. I'll just come over there when I'm done."

"Okay, but hurry. It's just not the same without you."

"You didn't even know me six weeks ago, Matthew Trevor."

"And now that I do, life's just not the same without you."

"Yeah," she actually giggled, "I know what you mean."

While Melody finished packing, it occurred to her that she should get something for Matthew's family as well. She said a quick prayer for guidance in her shopping. Her budget was limited, but she could manage if she found the right thing; she just didn't want to spend all day looking. She was grateful the snow had stopped in the night and the roads had been cleared. She wasn't nearly as confident as Matthew was about driving in bad weather.

Melody did feel guided in her purchases, but as she contemplated the reality that she was becoming a part of these people's lives, something formless tightened up inside of her. She thought back to the moment when she had known she should marry Matthew. She couldn't question that it was right, but that didn't take away the same old fears that erupted from the memories of her upbringing. She cussed aloud and hit the steering wheel, wondering why she couldn't be free of such thoughts—even long enough to enjoy Christmas. Then she got angry with herself for cussing. She figured it was tangible evidence that she hadn't gotten past the atmosphere she'd been raised in nearly as much as she would like to think.

Praying inwardly for help in overcoming her discouragement, and to be able to feel the spirit of Christmas and enjoy the holiday, Melody felt a little better as she made her last stop in downtown Provo. It took several minutes to find a parking place, and she almost gave up. But she had something in mind that she hoped would be worth the effort.

As Melody walked into the Hallmark store, she had to just stand there for a few minutes and absorb the atmosphere. She closed her eyes and could almost imagine herself in the center of a dream. Reminding herself of the time, she prayed for guidance and hurried to find one last thing for Matthew. She bought wrapping paper and cards, too. Then she drove to Matthew's house and hauled her packages into the spare bedroom, along with her overnight bag and her new dress, still hanging beneath the plastic cover they'd put over it in the store.

"I thought I saw you sneak in," Matthew said, startling her. Then he pulled her into his arms and kissed her with a trace of passion.

Melody absorbed the sensation, wishing she could be free of the subtle, nagging doubts that crept in against her will. Concentrating on the moment, she tried to push them away. When he drew back to look into her eyes, she said softly, "Will you kiss me like that every day for the rest of my life?"

"You can bet on it," he said and kissed her again. Then he just held her, wondering what life had been like before Melody.

Chapter Twelve

Matthew finally stepped back to put distance between himself and Melody, longing for the day when she would be his wife. "I asked Mom about bringing your mother to Christmas dinner," he said. "She told me that would be great."

"Are you sure?" Melody asked.

"Of course I'm sure."

"Okay, but . . . Matthew," she said, "I've been thinking about your idea—about the Nutcracker tickets. I really think it would be perfect. Can we call and see if there are any tickets available?"

"Sure. Let's do that now." He took her hand and led her to the kitchen, where Janna was rolling something up in a dishtowel covered with powdered sugar.

"What is that?" Melody asked. She'd gotten past trying to cover her ignorance with these people.

"It's a pumpkin cake roll," Janna explained. "After it cools, then we unroll it, spread it with a cream cheese filling, and roll it back up."

"Ooh, and it's heavenly," Matthew declared.

"I can't wait," Melody said dreamily.

"Hey, Mom, do you think it would still be possible to get Nutcracker tickets?"

"I don't know, but you could try."

"Do you have the number?" Matthew asked.

"Yes, I can get it in a minute," Janna said. "What's up. . . if you don't mind my asking?"

Matthew briefly explained what Melody had gotten her mother for Christmas, and why taking her to the Nutcracker would go perfectly with the new dress and shoes.

"I think that's a wonderful idea," Janna said, then more to Melody, "And I was glad to hear that you'll be bringing your mother to dinner tomorrow. We're looking forward to meeting her."

Melody managed a smile, hoping she wasn't getting into something that would cause problems. She felt somehow apprehensive about crossing her world with Matthew's any more than she already had.

"So, where's the number for the theater?" Matthew asked.

"I can get it in a minute," Janna said. "But . . . we have two extra tickets."

Matthew and Melody exchanged a quick glance. "We do?" Matthew asked.

"Well, Caitlin and Mallory have taken friends the last few years, so I bought two extra tickets. But this year neither of them had any friends available to go. They're either out of town or have other plans. So I was hoping we could find someone to use them. I thought of Melody already. But . . . well . . ." Janna smiled over her shoulder, "I guess that other ticket was meant for Melody's mother."

Matthew hummed a few bars of the theme song from *The Twilight Zone,* then he laughed. Melody smiled at him, saying, "I told you, you're the Christmas king."

"Hey, I got it from my mother," he said.

"And I got it from your father," Janna countered.

"Got what?" Colin asked, coming into the kitchen.

"I'm not sure," Melody said, "but I think they're talking about the spirit of Christmas."

"Well, wherever we got it, I'm glad we have it," Colin Trevor declared. Then he put an arm around Melody's shoulders, giving her a quick hug. "I hear a rumor that you're practically a member of the family."

Melody hated the way her heart quickened without warning, and she had to consciously will herself to not appear alarmed. A glance at Matthew made her doubtful that she'd covered it quickly enough.

"I heard that rumor, too." Melody forced a smile, holding up her left hand. Matthew's parents ooh'd and ah'd over the ring. Melody avoided Matthew's eyes. She felt as if he was attempting to read her thoughts.

"Well, I think it's great," Colin said. "You're a wonderful girl." He slapped Matthew playfully on the shoulder. "What's more, I don't think I've ever seen this kid so happy. And I've seen him pretty happy."

"You mean like the Christmas just after I'd turned seven?" Matthew asked, his concern apparently gone.

Colin smiled and took his wife's hand. "Yeah, that was a good one. Our first Christmas together."

Melody observed the serenity in their expressions. From the story Matthew had told her about his parents, she could well imagine what that Christmas might have been like.

"Hey," Matthew said, "why don't we wrap your mother's gifts and take them over."

"Okay," Melody said, not feeling the least bit apprehensive. While Matthew was looking for a box the right size to wrap a ticket in, Melody called her mother to tell her they were coming over a little later. Then she locked the door to the room she was using and hurried to wrap the gifts she had purchased.

"Are you nervous?" Matthew asked in the car.

"No, just excited."

"We've come a long way."

"Yes," she said with light sarcasm, "and it's been such a long time."

"Well, actually we've known each other for zillions of years. That's why we fell in love so quickly. We already loved each other before we were ever born."

"Does that mean we were in love when we were angels?"

"Yes, I think that's what it means."

"That's a nice thought," Melody said. It actually helped her believe she could get beyond this smoldering anxiety.

They stopped at Sister Thompson's house first and had a nice visit. The old woman told them her son would be coming to get her soon, and she would be staying with his family for the next few days. She was delighted to hear of their engagement, and she got tears in her eyes when Melody invited her to attend the temple ceremony. "That's the best Christmas present I've ever gotten," Sister Thompson said.

"Well, you did take her to Primary," Matthew interjected.

They left when Sister Thompson's son arrived, and Melody actually felt excited to see her mother. She was relieved to arrive at the house and find the front room void of anyone but Thelma Morgan. She seemed a little down, but greeted them with a smile and invited them in, telling Matthew it was nice to see him again. And the house didn't even look too bad.

"Oh, my," Thelma said when Melody handed her the gift, wrapped in brightly colored paper with a huge red bow. "What on earth is this for?"

"It's for Christmas, Mother."

"But . . . ," Thelma began, then she didn't seem to know what to say.

"Just open it," Melody said as she and Matthew sat on the couch.

Thelma sat at the edge of a chair, seeming flustered and uncertain. "I . . . I don't know what to say. I . . . can't remember the last time I . . ."

"Just open it, Mother," Melody repeated, taking Matthew's hand. They exchanged a warm glance, and she could see that he was almost as excited as she was.

Thelma carefully removed the bow and set it aside as if she would save it forever. She did the same with the paper. Then she gingerly lifted the box lid, folded back the tissue, and froze—the same way Melody froze when she had opened her new coat. And then Thelma Morgan cried.

Matthew had the urge to cry himself as he observed Melody hugging her mother. She pulled the dress out of the box and held it up for Thelma to see. And Thelma cried harder, managing to say, "It's the most beautiful thing I've ever owned. I can't believe it." Melody pointed out the shoes in the bottom of the box, and Thelma put a hand over her mouth.

Matthew figured this was a good time to step in. He pulled the little flat box from his coat pocket and handed it to Thelma. "Now, we wouldn't want you to be all dressed up and have nowhere to go," he said. Thelma met his eyes for a long moment before she tentatively reached out to take the package. Again she got tears in her eyes as she stared at the ticket, listening to Melody explain how they were going to take her to the Nutcracker ballet.

"Matthew told me the theater is beautiful. It's in downtown Salt Lake City, and they have a live orchestra. His mother said we have some of the best seats in the house, so we'll be able to see it really well."

"Oh, I can't believe it," Thelma said again.

"And . . . ," Matthew drawled as a preamble to the next portion of their surprise, "my parents asked me to extend an invitation to spend Christmas dinner with us tomorrow. If it's all right with you, we'll pick you up at about one, and we'll expect you to be wearing that dress."

Thelma stared at him in disbelief for a full minute before she squeaked, "But why would . . ." Again she couldn't seem to find the words.

"Well, my parents really want to meet you, Mrs. Morgan. And before we get into that, there's something I need to ask you."

Melody looked over at him in surprise. She hadn't expected this. But Matthew's focus was completely on Thelma. He took her hand into his and looked into her eyes, saying softly, "I would like to ask for your blessing, Mrs. Morgan. I've asked Melody to marry me."

Thelma took a sharp breath and briefly glanced at Melody, as if to say this was all too good to be true. "Well . . . of course," Thelma said. "Of course you have my blessing. I'm flattered that you even asked. It's apparent that you're a nice young man." Thelma looked again at Melody, then back to Matthew. "And she'll make a good wife, my Melody. She's the strong one, you know. Of all my children, she's the one I knew would amount to something. I knew it the moment she was born. There was always something different about her."

Matthew glanced at Melody. "Yes, she's something special, all right."

The three of them visited for about twenty minutes before Melody's brother, Joe, emerged from the back of the house to turn on the television. Melody quickly introduced him to Matthew and decided this would be a good time to leave.

On their way out to the car, Matthew said, "He was a little nicer than Ben."

"He was less drunk at the moment," Melody said.

After they drove for a few minutes in silence, Melody turned to Matthew and said, "I think that was absolutely one of the best moments of my life."

Matthew smiled and kissed her hand. "Mine too, if you must know the truth."

"And I'm not even going to think about what my brothers and sisters are doing for Christmas," Melody said. "I don't even want to know."

"Maybe we could work on that next year."

"Maybe," she said, her eyes becoming distant.

"Hey," Matthew reminded her, "they made their choices. You made yours."

"I know," she agreed. "And I'm doing better with that. It's just . . ."

"You said you weren't going to think about it. Remember them in your prayers and enjoy the holiday, okay?"

Melody smiled and kissed *his* hand. "Okay."

"Forgive me if I'm being presumptuous," Matthew said, "but you seem awfully tense when the subject of a wedding comes up."

Melody turned to look at him, wanting to tell him he had no idea what he was talking about. But she was too consumed with shock over his perception to say anything at all.

"Well?" he pressed. "At first I was thinking that maybe my parents make you a little nervous. But you were the same at Sister Thompson's—and with your mother."

They had arrived at his house, and Melody was hoping they could just go inside and postpone this conversation. But Matthew put the car in park and made it clear he wasn't moving until she answered his question. She quickly searched for a response that would be honest without getting into the full depth of her feelings.

"It's just . . . so fast, Matthew. I guess I'm having trouble adjusting."

"I can understand that, but . . ."

"Matthew, it's Christmas. Let's enjoy the holiday and—"

"I can't enjoy the holiday if I think something's bothering you. Let's just talk about it now and—"

Melody breathed an audible sigh of relief as Matthew's little brothers ran out to the car to get them. Janna had told them they couldn't start their celebrations until Matthew and Melody returned, and they were anxious.

Matthew helped Melody out of the car and started toward the door, but he stopped just outside, saying, "Can we talk later?"

Melody nodded reluctantly. What else could she do?

The family gathered to share a meal and clean up the kitchen, then they moved to the family room to read the Christmas story from the Bible. Melody became caught up in the warm spirit that hovered around her and forgot all about the thoughts that had been troubling her. With Matthew's arm around her, everything was perfect—for the moment.

As Melody watched the children hang their stockings on the mantel over a large fireplace in the family room, she felt a sensation that had become recently familiar. If not for tangible evidence that she was awake and breathing, she might believe this was all a dream.

"Hang your stocking, Matthew," Dustin said, handing it to him.

"I thought I was too old for that," he protested lightly.

"Never," his mother said with drama.

"And neither is Melody," Colin added, presenting her with a Christmas stocking similar to Matthew's. It was made out of brightly colored Christmas fabric, obviously homemade.

To avoid crying, Melody laughed. "Wow! My very own Christmas stocking. That is so neat! Thank you."

She hung her stocking on a little hook next to Matthew's. Then he kissed her quickly and whispered, "Merry Christmas."

With that done, Colin gathered everyone together for family prayer. Melody had heard about such things for years in her church meetings, but once again, she was experiencing something for the first time. She felt perhaps more in awe of this than any other Christmas ritual they had participated in. Something tangibly warm consumed her as Matthew took her hand and they knelt with his family. Colin asked Matthew to give the prayer. As she listened to this man she had grown to love pray aloud on behalf of his family, that dreamlike sensation intensified. It all just seemed too good to be true—which was, perhaps, the very reason for her doubts.

Melody found the antics of getting the children to go to bed rather humorous. Janna didn't seem to think so. They were all excited and full of energy, and she'd obviously had a busy day, with many things still to accomplish. Colin intervened and got the children settled down.

Matthew asked his mother if they could help, and she gladly put them to work in her bedroom wrapping gifts. They talked and laughed as they wrapped toys, clothes, books, and a number of other miscellaneous items. While Melody certainly didn't begrudge the abundance of Christmas for this family, how could she not compare it to the lack of Christmas in her own life? She wondered how her father could have been so callous and unfeeling. It wasn't the lack of gifts and material things that Melody resented in her upbringing. It was the lack of love; the absence of any effort to bring something good into the lives of his children. Melody believed that her mother had a good heart, but it had been wrapped in barbed wire by a man who had claimed to be a husband and father. The entire thing was horribly tragic. Melody knew all of that was in the past. But the repercussions were still with her—and even more so for her siblings. It was all so sad.

Of course, Melody had been immensely blessed. The evidence was all around her. She was spending Christmas with a wonderful family, and she was engaged to a wonderful man. But that was just one more thing that concerned her.

"Hey, where are you?" Matthew asked, startling her.

"I'm right here," she smiled, grateful that his mother was in the room with them. The last thing she wanted to talk about now was her family; or worse, the way she couldn't get past these nagging doubts. How could she possibly explain these feelings to Matthew and have him understand?

"While you're finishing these," Janna said, indicating the few remaining gifts, "I'm going to go help your father with a little project in the garage."

Melody wanted to shout *Don't leave us alone*! But Matthew almost smirked as his mother left the room and closed the door. "Now we can talk," he said.

"About what?" She figured pretending innocence couldn't hurt.

"Something's bothering you, Melody," he stated.

"I'm having a wonderful time, Matthew. There's absolutely no reason on earth why I shouldn't be the happiest woman alive."

"But something's bothering you," he repeated.

She said nothing.

"Melody," Matthew lowered his voice and leaned toward her, "you can talk to me. I'm the man you're going to marry. I would hope that means I'm also your best friend."

Melody had to admit, "You're the only real friend I've got."

"Then talk to me."

"But . . . it's Christmas Eve. I just want to enjoy the holiday and not—"

"Melody, if something's bothering you, I'm not going to ignore it. We can't make a marriage work if we can't communicate."

"Well . . . that's just it, Matthew."

"What?" he pressed when she said nothing more.

Tears threatened as Melody got closer to the truth. "I'm scared, Matthew," she finally admitted, realizing he wasn't going to let up.

"Scared?" This was not what he'd expected. "Of what?"

"What?" she echoed. "I don't even know where to begin."

Matthew listened with increasing uneasiness as Melody poured her fears into his lap. It all came down to one point. She was afraid that her upbringing would interfere with her ability to make a marriage work. A part of her just didn't believe she could overcome the past enough to be a good wife and mother.

When she finally ran down, Matthew asked gently, "Haven't you been paying attention, Melody? Haven't you seen where my mother has come from? Everything you need to make a good life is already inside of you, and I know that with—"

"How can you know that when *I* don't know it? Your mother is a remarkable woman, Matthew, and I don't question that she's risen above a lot and come a long way. But she didn't grow up under the same roof with a raving maniac."

"No, but I did!"

"But you got out when you were six, Matthew. You've seen how marriage is supposed to work—day in and day out." She jumped to her feet and started pacing. "What have I seen? Seventeen years of anger and shouting, Matthew. Day after day after day. Do you think that hasn't left an impression on me? How do you think I'm going to respond the first time one of my children gets sassy with me? Or what if you come home in a bad mood, and I just can't handle it? You don't know me as well as you think you do, Matthew Trevor."

Matthew leaned back and folded his arms, determined to let her rant until she got it out of her system.

"Do you know what I do when I'm alone?" she continued. "If I stub my toe or drop something, eight out of ten times, foul words just jump out of my mouth. I do better than I used to, but it's a weakness I struggle with every day of my life. The fact is, I spent the majority of my life in a home where those words flew back and forth in every sentence. What are you going to do if your kids start cussing? But they didn't learn those words at school; they heard them in the kitchen, while Mom was cooking dinner. Am I getting through to you here?"

"Loud and clear," Matthew said. "Now, why don't you sit down and listen to what *I* have to say."

Melody did as he asked. If nothing else, the fact that he had remained perfectly composed while she'd been yelling had a calming effect.

"I cannot promise you perfect peace and bliss, Melody. I cannot promise you that we won't have differences. And I cannot promise you that I'll never get angry. But I *can* promise you this: I will always be there. You and I have the gospel, Melody, and we have the keys to know how to use it. I know in my heart that as long as we keep that foremost in our relationship, we can make it through anything."

"And what if we don't? What if one of us slips?"

"Then I guess we'll have some lessons to learn the hard way." He lifted a finger toward her. "Has it occurred to you that maybe you're creating problems where they don't even exist? Has it ever crossed your mind that maybe—just maybe—you are a strong, capable woman who has the ability to overcome anything she sets her mind to?"

"Yeah, well maybe not!" Melody shouted quietly, just wanting to be angry. But looking into Matthew's eyes softened her. She looked away, hoping to hide the emotion that was suddenly too intense to ignore. "I'm just so afraid that I'll hurt you, Matthew; that I won't be able to meet your expectations, or—"

"Listen to me." Matthew took hold of her arm. "I came home from school one day when I was ten and found out that my mother had kicked my father out of the house. The details aren't important. The bottom line? She was being abusive, and he was being codependent. The problems finally blew up like a match thrown in a gasoline spill. My parents were separated for about a year and a half. My mother had a breakdown; she's told you about that, I believe. But maybe what you don't realize is that *I* was there. I saw my father cry every time she refused to see him. In every prayer he ever uttered, I heard him beg for his family to be put back together. Do you have any comprehension of the joy we felt when that happened? Do you know how many times in the years since that I have heard them say how grateful they are to be together? That's what *I* grew up seeing, Melody, and by heaven and earth, I *will* be with you forever." He finished with his fists clenched and his teeth clamped tightly.

Matthew's heart began to pound as he watched Melody silently staring at nothing. He could almost feel her mind spinning, and he wondered if he could bear having her call off the engagement, now that they'd come this far.

"Do you want to tell me what's on your mind?" he finally asked, unable to bear it another second.

"Not really, but I suppose I should."

Matthew sighed and pushed his head into his hands. "I can't force you to marry me, Melody. I can't force you to be happy."

"I know that," she said. "And that's why I need some time. I told you I'd marry you, and I believe in my heart it's the right thing to do." Matthew looked up at her. Maybe this wasn't as bad as he'd expected. "But I have to be ready. There are just . . . some things I need . . . to come to terms with, I guess. Be patient with me. That's all I ask."

Matthew reminded himself of what he'd told her when he'd proposed. "It's like I said, Mel, I've got forever."

Melody immersed herself in his embrace. "I'm sorry, Matthew. I didn't want to ruin your Christmas or—"

"You haven't ruined anybody's Christmas, Melody. Maybe you should look at how far you've come, instead of how far you have to go."

Melody looked up into his eyes, marveling at his acceptance and wisdom.

"Hey," he added with a little smirk, "when I met you, you were the president of the anti-Christmas society. Now you're actually concerned about *enjoying* Christmas."

Melody laughed softly and hugged him again.

Figuring a distraction would work wonders, Matthew declared, "It's almost midnight. We've got work to do."

"We do? I was thinking more about getting some sleep."

"Oh, not yet! It's Christmas Eve. You can sleep anytime."

They hurried to finish wrapping the gifts Janna had left, then Matthew took Melody's hand and led her quietly to the kids' bedrooms. She expected them to be sleeping, but as they leaned close to each door, they could hear whispering and giggling. She then followed Matthew on what he called a "Santa Claus excursion." She refused to follow him up to the roof, but she did ring the jingle bells while he stomped around up there.

When he climbed down he was chuckling. "That ought to get those little cookie snitchers going."

"Now they'll *never* sleep," Melody said.

"Nah, they'll be so scared that Santa will catch them awake, they won't make a sound."

Matthew kissed her and the bells in her hand jingled as she pushed her arms around his shoulders. He drew back and grinned. "I told you I'd have you ringing jingle bells."

Melody smiled. "So you did. I guess I should believe what you tell me."

Matthew recalled their most recent conversation and added, "Yes, you should."

They went quietly into the house and found Janna artistically arranging wrapped gifts around the tree while Colin filled stockings. Matthew and Melody cuddled up on the couch to watch until Melody drifted to sleep, feeling again as if she was living in a dream. She was vaguely aware of Matthew guiding her to the spare bedroom and tucking her into the bed. She opened her eyes for a moment and saw the image of her angel hero, standing at the foot of the bed, keeping his silent vigil on her behalf. She blinked and realized that it was Matthew, silhouetted against the hall light.

"I love you," he whispered and closed the door. Melody nuzzled into the bed and drifted back to sleep. She'd never felt so perfectly safe and happy in her life. *She only prayed that it would last.*

Melody's next awareness was Matthew's lips against hers. "Wake up, gorgeous," he whispered. "It's Christmas."

She groaned and pulled the covers over her head, but Matthew told her she had five minutes to get up and make herself presentable.

"Or what?" she asked.

He laughed like a villain in a melodrama. "You just wait and see. We could start by seeing where you're ticklish."

Melody decided that getting up would be her best option. She had seen the way he tickled his brothers and sisters, and she'd simply rather not endure it—especially with his family around.

It didn't take Melody long to get caught up in the Christmas morning frenzy, while that dream-like sensation hovered around her. It was difficult not to feel a little heartache for her own childhood as she observed the children opening their gifts and digging into their stockings. But she concentrated on the moment, forcing every unhappy thought from her mind.

The cookie jar that crowed was a big hit. Janna and Colin laughed so hard they got tears in their eyes. Matthew leaned over to Melody and whispered, "I told you they'd love it."

Melody was grateful she'd had the insight to get the family a gift, though it seemed insignificant compared to the many gifts she received. She was in awe and humbled by the love and acceptance she had received from these people, and the effort they had gone to on her behalf. At one point she quietly told Matthew, "This is hard for me to accept so much when—"

"Melody," he whispered, looking directly into her eyes, "you have given my family a great deal of joy in the opportunity to share Christmas with you. Giving gifts is not about giving as much as you receive, or about comparisons." He touched her nose with his finger. "Just relax and enjoy yourself."

Melody nodded and hugged him tightly, reminding herself to be gracious and let go of her pride.

Together, Matthew's parents opened the gift Melody had gotten for the family. It was gratifying to see the genuine emotion in their eyes–especially Janna's. "It's beautiful," she said, examining the large snow globe set on an oak base.

"It somehow reminded me of . . . being in your home," Melody said. Janna actually got tears in her eyes as Colin turned the globe to make the snow fall over the little nativity scene, complete with an angel hovering above the stable.

"Oh, and there's a music box," Janna said, noticing the

key in the bottom. "It plays a Christmas melody," she added as it began to tinkle a medley of Christmas songs.

Matthew chuckled. When it seemed he was the only one who had picked up on it, he said, "That's why it's the perfect gift from Melody."

When all the gifts had been opened, Melody helped gather the scraps of wrapping paper and pick up the mess. Setting all of her gifts together, she noticed she'd forgotten something. Everyone else was preoccupied when Melody handed Matthew another small gift.

"What is this?" he asked.

"It's a Christmas present," she stated.

He smirked. "I can see that, but—"

"Just be gracious and open it."

While Melody watched him tear the paper away, she recalled their conversation last night concerning her fears for the future. She hoped he knew this gift was an expression of her hope for getting beyond it.

Matthew felt an unexpected surge of emotion when he uncovered the Christmas ornament they had once looked at together in the Hallmark store. "Our first Christmas together," he read aloud, then he looked into her eyes. "I'd forgotten all about this."

"You told me I should buy it for you."

"So I did. And you actually went into that sweet, cozy little store to buy this for me. I thought you hated that store."

"I did. But some things change."

Matthew hugged her tightly. "Thank you, Mel. I love it. May the next fifty-seven Christmases together be so good."

Melody pushed away the habitual tension she felt at the thought of actually, really getting married. She reminded herself to enjoy the present and gave him a kiss.

Chapter Thirteen

Melody helped bring a semblance of order to the family room, then she helped Janna in the kitchen until it was nearly time to go get her mother. In the spare bedroom she changed into her new dress. Looking at herself in the long mirror on the back of the door, she could hardly believe it was her. Had Matthew Trevor changed her life so drastically? Or had the changes within herself come so gradually that she hadn't noticed? Perhaps a little of both. She felt certain that Matthew's love had brought out the best in her. It was a thought which made having a future with him seem so right—if she could only get past this nagging fear.

When Melody walked into the front room where Matthew was waiting for her, he looked up and drew in a long breath. His eyes sparkled as he said, "That's what a Christmas baby is supposed to look like when she's all grown up."

Melody and Matthew arrived to pick Thelma up at one o'clock. She answered the door wearing her new dress, her coat slung over her arm. Melody couldn't remember the last time she'd seen her mother's hair curled, and she was actually wearing a touch of makeup. But more important, Thelma Morgan was beaming—as if this was her first date.

"Oh," she said to Melody as they walked toward the car, "did you get a new coat?"

"Matthew gave it to me for my birthday."

"He's got good taste," Thelma said.

"Yes, I do," Matthew agreed, smirking toward Melody.

Thelma chattered excitedly as they drove. But by the time they arrived at the Trevors' house, she had become very quiet. Melody could almost imagine her mother's thoughts as they drove into the nice neighborhood on the east bench of Provo, and into the driveway. Melody had felt much the same way the first time she'd come here. Except that Melody had previously discovered life beyond the confinement of the home she'd grown up in. But she wondered how long it had been since Thelma Morgan had gone anywhere beyond the doctor's office and the grocery store.

"Are you nervous, Mother?" Melody asked while Matthew was walking around the car to open the door.

"I believe I am."

"It's okay. I was nervous the first time I came here, too. But they're wonderful people. And they're going to love you."

Thelma looked at her daughter in disbelief, then she allowed Matthew to help her out of the car.

Melody was not surprised, but perhaps awed by the way Colin and Janna Trevor took Thelma Morgan into their home. They fussed over her and made clever conversation, even when Thelma would hardly speak. She observed her surroundings as if she had suddenly awakened in a time warp.

When Melody offered to help Janna in the kitchen, Thelma followed, as if she needed to stay close to her daughter. At first Janna tried to insist that Thelma didn't need to help, but when Thelma was put to work stirring a pan of gravy while it thickened, she seemed to relax a little.

"You have a beautiful home," Thelma commented to Janna.

"Oh, it is nice," Janna agreed. "But I can't take much credit. Colin bought it while I was in the hospital having a nervous breakdown."

Thelma stopped stirring and looked up at Janna as if she'd suddenly turned purple. She seemed to expect some evidence that Janna was joking. Then she glanced at Melody, as if to question this interesting revelation.

"Of course, these things happen," Janna went on casually while she arranged pickles and olives on a tray. Thelma started stirring again. "I guess it was inevitable after what I'd been through, but it was still a tough time for all of us."

Janna noticed that the gravy was boiling and turned off the burner. She handed a bowl to Thelma, saying, "Would you mind pouring that in there? Thank you. Anyway, where was I? Oh, yes, we were talking about when Colin bought the house. He had to take care of the kids, of course. I wasn't any good to them at the time." Janna stopped what she was doing and looked at Thelma as if they were the best of friends. "Have you ever just felt like you were so out of control that the walls were going to fall in on you? Well, that's how it was. And finally I just couldn't take it anymore."

Melody observed her future mother-in-law with growing admiration. With all the time she'd spent in Janna Trevor's home, she'd never known her to be a chatterbox—until now. The reason was obvious: she had something to say that she wanted Thelma Morgan to hear, and Thelma was obviously too nervous to participate in casual conversation.

"Anyway," Janna went on, "I really had a hard time feeling guilty and all. But I finally realized that the way I felt was understandable. I mean . . . the things my father did to me were unspeakable. And then, my first husband . . . he was a raving maniac. I don't know if there's anything more terrifying than living with a man you just can't predict. And when they start raging, it's hell, don't you think, Thelma?"

Thelma nodded mechanically, seeming dazed. She almost looked as if she might cry.

"Well," Janna glanced around, "I think we're about ready to eat."

"Uh . . . ," Thelma finally made a noise, "could I use . . ."

"The bathroom's just around the corner," Melody pointed.

After Thelma left the room, Janna popped an olive in her mouth and said to Melody, "Do you think I overdid it?"

Melody smiled. "I think you were perfect."

"Well," Janna chuckled, "I was trying to be inspired. Maybe your mother and I can have a *real* conversation about it sometime when she warms up a little. In the meantime, I just wanted her to know that we had something in common."

Melody impulsively hugged Janna, then she helped set dinner on the table. Taking note of the beautiful meal spread before them, combined with the events of the holiday to this point, Melody was reminded of a scene from *A Christmas Carol*. The Ghost of Christmas Present had come with an abundance of the good things of the world, and Melody found evidence of that here. But it occurred to her that the true joy in their celebration was the warm spirit of love and giving.

Thelma came out of the bathroom just as the glazed ham was being set out. Matthew escorted her to a chair next to Melody and helped her with it. When the family was seated, Colin stood at the head of the table and offered a blessing on the food. In the prayer he expressed gratitude for the opportunity to celebrate Christ's birth with such abundance, and among loved ones. He became emotional as he thanked their Father in Heaven for keeping his family together in spite of the adversity in their lives. He also uttered thanks for having Melody and her mother with them, and for the sweet spirit these special women brought into their home. When Melody felt Matthew squeeze her hand beneath the table, she reached for her mother's hand and did the same.

Through the meal, Thelma said very little. Melody sensed her awe and nervousness, realizing that her mother's feelings were similar to those Melody had experienced on Thanksgiving Day. She was amazed at how far she had come in so short a time.

When the meal was finished, Thelma seemed to relax. She offered to help in the kitchen and Janna gladly accepted, providing Thelma with an apron to protect her dress. While Janna put the food away, Mallory and Caitlin cleared the table, and Matthew loaded the dishwasher. Thelma dug in and started washing pans, Melody dried dishes, and Colin put them away. Still, Thelma didn't say much, but she seemed to enjoy listening to the bantering and laughter going on around her.

When the kitchen was in order, Janna announced, "I'm not cooking anymore until next year. There's a fridge full of leftovers. You guys are on your own."

She spread out an assortment of Christmas goodies on the dining room table to be enjoyed through the remainder of the day, then the adults gathered in the front room.

Melody sat on the floor near the angel tree, and Matthew lay down with his head in her lap, declaring he needed a nap. During a quiet moment Thelma said, "I have a little something for you, Melody. It's not much, but . . ." She reached into her purse as she spoke. "It's something I've always had in mind to give you. And I think the time is right."

Matthew sat up and became attentive as Thelma handed Melody a small, flat package wrapped in white tissue paper. Melody took the gift from her mother, but hesitated to open it.

"Go on," Thelma urged. "As I said, it's not much, but . . ."

Melody opened the package to find a lacy white handkerchief. "It's beautiful," Melody said, but her eyes were questioning as she glanced toward her mother.

Thelma leaned forward, saying, "When I was a young woman, twelve or thirteen, I think, a fine lady who lived around the corner gave that to me. I don't remember her name, or what the occasion might have been. But she told me I should take it with me when I married in the temple."

Melody managed to keep from gasping, but she could feel a knot tightening somewhere between her heart and her stomach.

"Of course," Thelma chuckled with no trace of humor, "I ended up pregnant at seventeen and . . . well, I never made it to the temple. But I always hoped that one day you would . . ." Tears gathered in Thelma's eyes. "I want you to take that with you when you get married, Melody. And even though I can't be with you . . ." She became too emotional to speak, and an uncomfortable silence hung in the air. Thelma gave another humorless chuckle and finished, "I always knew you would amount to something. You were always the strong one."

Melody moved to her mother's side and hugged her tightly. "Thank you, Mother. I'll treasure it always." She looked into Thelma's eyes, adding, "I love you."

Thelma nodded as if to echo the sentiment, then she dug into her purse for a tissue. The tension was broken when Janna said, "Well, Thelma, it would seem that you and I have a great deal in common." Thelma looked surprised but interested. "I, too, was unwed and pregnant at seventeen."

"Now, I find that difficult to believe," Thelma said, seeming more comfortable than she had since she'd arrived. "What kind of scoundrel took advantage of a sweet little thing like you?"

Matthew chuckled, while Melody became alarmed. Janna just smiled. And Colin admitted with a little grin, "Uh . . . that would be me."

"Oh, my," Thelma seemed embarrassed. "Forgive me. I had no idea that—"

"It's all right," Colin assured her, "I think we got over the embarrassment of that a long time ago. As you can see," he motioned toward Matthew, "the results weren't too bad in the long run."

"Well, you have a fine son, that's apparent," Thelma said. "And you've obviously raised a good family." She added more to Janna, "You got lucky, my dear. I think we might have done all right if my Roy hadn't been such a drinker. But, well. . . his father before him was the same way. And his grandfather, too."

"We're very blessed that way," Janna said. "Alcoholism is *one* problem we haven't struggled with. But we've had our fair share of difficulties."

"You mentioned that earlier," Thelma said. "I must say I'm surprised. I always thought that people with such problems didn't stand much of a chance to get past it."

"Well, it's not easy," Janna said, "but I owe most of the credit to the Lord. Between divine intervention and a good husband, we made it through." Janna smiled at Colin and he kissed her hand, much the way Matthew often kissed Melody's.

"You're lucky there," Thelma said. "I wish I could say that my Roy had been worth a hill of beans."

Melody couldn't recall her mother ever speaking so openly. But then, perhaps she'd never had the opportunity to express her feelings before. Melody caught a sly smile from Janna and felt certain that her rambling in the kitchen about her breakdown and abuse had paid off.

The conversation moved on to other things, and Thelma seemed to be enjoying herself. Janna brought out photo albums and the women made a fuss over pictures of Matthew as a child, while Matthew and Colin napped on the floor. When they started looking at pictures Matthew had sent home from his mission, he got up and said, "I think that's enough home movies for one day, Mother. You'll scare them away."

"I thought you were asleep," Melody protested as he took the album and set it aside.

"With all that cackling going on? Are you kidding?"

He laughed and Janna suggested, "Why don't the two of you show Thelma the tree downstairs, and I'll fix some hot chocolate."

"What an excellent idea," Matthew said, and surprised Thelma by taking her hand to lead her down the stairs. He talked to her about the significance of many of the ornaments on the tree, and Melody was fascinated as much by Matthew's attentiveness as she was by her mother's childlike awe.

When Thelma declared that she needed to get home, Janna fixed her an enormous plate of assorted goodies to take and share with her family. Thelma expressed her gratitude for everything several times, and Janna promised to have her over again soon.

In the car, Thelma said, "I hope I didn't say anything to embarrass you—either of you. I'm not used to being around such fine people." Turning to Matthew, she said, "It was nice knowing your family's had some struggles, too, I must admit. But I'm afraid I might have said too much."

"Nonsense," Matthew assured her. "Having you with us was a delight. We'll have to make a tradition of it."

Melody hugged her mother at the door, not wanting to go inside. They made arrangements to pick her up on the afternoon of the thirtieth for the ballet. Thelma thanked Melody profusely for such a wonderful Christmas, and Melody thanked her mother for the beautiful handkerchief. They hugged again, then Matthew impulsively hugged Thelma as well.

"You take care now. . . *Mother,*" he said with a little smirk. "We'll see you in a few days." Thelma nearly blushed as she waved and went into the house.

Back in the car, Melody took Matthew's hand. "Thank you," she said. "She's probably never been treated so well a day in her life."

Matthew pressed Melody's hand to his lips. "She's your mother, Mel. For that reason alone, she deserves my respect."

Melody wished she could tell him how much that meant to her.

Melody was glad that Matthew took her back to his house. She didn't want the day to end. They walked in to find the youngsters all busy with their new games and toys, with a few of their friends hanging around. After changing back into comfortable clothes, Melody and Matthew found Janna and Colin sitting at the dining room table, feeding each other tidbits of Christmas goodies and laughing like children.

"You got your mother home safely, I take it," Colin said.

"Oh, yes. She had a wonderful time."

"She's very sweet," Janna added. "We enjoyed having her here." She squeezed Melody's hand across the table. "And I mean that."

Melody smiled. "I want you to know how much I appreciate your effort to take her in like that, and to let her know that you've had your own struggles. I would guess it means almost as much to her as it does to me." Melody took Matthew's hand. "I know it sounds strange, but you can't imagine the comfort it's given me to know that Matthew has gone through some similar challenges. Well . . . I know the circumstances varied a lot, but I think he understands how I feel . . . and that means a great deal."

"It would seem the two of you were meant for each other," Janna said.

In her heart, Melody believed that was true. If she could only get past a more logical part of herself that seemed to be trying to convince her otherwise.

"Well, what now?" Matthew asked.

"I don't know. Is there some silly Christmas video we haven't seen yet?"

"We could probably find something." Matthew stood and pulled her along.

Before they left the dining room, Melody impulsively leaned over to hug Janna.

"What was that for?" Janna laughed softly.

Without answering, Melody turned to Colin and opened her arms. He stood and embraced her, and she couldn't hold back her emotion as she looked into Judge Trevor's eyes. "Thank you," she said.

"For what?" Colin asked, baffled.

Melody turned to include Janna in her expressions of gratitude. "For being human, and for not being too proud to let me know that you've had your struggles. You can't imagine what that means to me. And thank you for taking me into your home without question or judgment."

Janna hugged Melody again and Colin put an arm around her, squeezing her shoulders. Their gestures expressed more acceptance than words ever could.

About twenty minutes into the movie *White Christmas,* Melody found her thoughts suddenly wandering with no explanation. Matthew noticed her brow furrow with apparent concern. "Is something wrong?" he asked.

Melody looked up at him as if she'd been startled. "I think I need to call my mother."

Matthew's heart quickened as he recalled Melody telling him that she'd found peace in severing her ties with her family because the Spirit had let her know she would be prompted if any need arose.

"Okay," he said, motioning toward the phone.

Melody quickly dialed the number, hoping for some minor problem that was typical of her household. One of the boys was probably drunk and broke something or took some money. But the moment Thelma answered the phone with a tense "Hello," Melody knew something was terribly wrong. She could hear shouting in the background.

"Mom? Are you okay?"

"Melody? Oh, thank heaven you called."

"What is it? What's wrong?"

While it was difficult to understand Thelma, Melody was able to get the gist of the problem. "Okay, Mom, we'll be right over," she said as calmly as she could.

Matthew stood up to go, but Melody dialed the phone again. "What are you doing?" he asked.

"I'm calling the police. From what I heard in the background, I'm not going over there unless the police are there first."

They hurried upstairs, and Matthew grabbed their coats while Melody gave his parents a ten-second explanation.

"You be careful," Janna said in alarm.

"Do you want me to go along?" Colin asked.

"No," Melody said, kissing his cheek, "but thank you. We'll call."

"So, what is it?" Matthew asked when they were in the car.

"Something to do with Lydia. Her boyfriend was there, obviously drunk, or stoned—or both. I only know there was a lot of yelling and screaming going on. And Mom said something about him hurting her."

"Her?"

"Lydia."

While Matthew drove quickly and carefully, Melody considered what was happening and groaned aloud. "Ooh, it's just like them to ruin one of the best days of my life. Do they plan it this way? I mean, I would swear my family lived by Murphy's Law."

"Hey," Matthew squeezed her hand, "our celebrations weren't interrupted. The last few days have been great."

"Yes, I know," she admitted.

"It could be worse," Matthew said.

"Don't say that until we get there and assess the damages."

Matthew and Melody arrived a few minutes after the police had left. Lydia was curled up on the couch, crying hysterically, her head in Thelma's lap. The police had arrested Lydia's boyfriend, Gary, when they'd entered the house to find him completely out of control. He'd hit Lydia more than once, then Ben—who was actually sober—had intervened. Ben reported that the police had also found drugs in Gary's possession.

"Well, at least that takes care of him for a while," Melody said. Then she touched the dried blood on her brother's lip. "Looks like he got you, too."

"Aw, it's nothing," Ben insisted. "I just hope Lyddie's all right."

Melody found Ben's concern a bit redeeming on his behalf. She knelt beside Lydia and took her hand. "Are you going to be all right?" she asked, noting that one side of her face was red and swollen.

Lydia only cried and muttered something incomprehensible. Melody was surprised when Matthew provided her with some ice wrapped in a dishtowel for Lydia's face. She wondered how far he'd had to dig to find a clean dishtowel, and what kind of disaster he might have encountered. "Thank you," she said. Their eyes met for only a second, but she hoped he knew how much she appreciated his support. Matthew smiled, then sat down with Ben, who seemed to be waiting for something to happen.

While Melody was trying to talk to Lydia with little success, Matthew commented to Ben, "So this Gary guy sounds like a real winner."

"Oh yeah," Ben said with the same sarcasm. "If he ever shows his face here again, I'm gonna beat the hell out of him, if I don't kill him first." Then he added, using some rather colorful language, that nothing upset him more than having the women in his family get hurt. Matthew studied Ben's expression and wondered if there was some hidden message intended for him. Was Ben wondering if Melody's boyfriend was going to hurt Melody the way Lydia's boyfriend had hurt her? Matthew almost laughed at the comparison.

While Ben and Matthew were chatting, Melody came to the conclusion that Lydia was just plain too upset to communicate *anything*. Melody finally turned to Thelma, who was wiping at a steady stream of tears. "What happened, Mom? Why is she so upset?"

"Well . . . it all started when she went into labor."

"She's in *labor?*" Melody almost shrieked.

Matthew and Ben perked up at that, moving closer as Thelma explained what had happened. When Lydia had started having regular contractions, she'd called Gary to tell him she was in labor. Through Thelma's rambling, it became evident that Lydia's biggest reason for wanting this baby was her hope that she could somehow win Gary's heart and some kind of a commitment. She was hopelessly in love with the jerk, apparently blind to his true character. Gary had come over in response to Lydia's call, but not to take her to the hospital. He'd immediately started shouting at her, telling her that he'd never wanted the baby, that he'd told her to abort it right at the start. He told Lydia he had no intention of supporting a baby or having anything to do with it; if she had ever thought otherwise, she was a fool. And if she was going to try to manipulate him like that, he had no intention of ever seeing her again.

"Of course, those weren't his exact words," Thelma said, and Lydia cried harder.

"I don't want to hear his exact words, Mother," Melody insisted, certain that Gary's language was not something she'd want to be exposed to.

"Well, then he hit her," Thelma added. "And that's about when you called."

"Is she still having contractions?" Melody asked.

"Well, I've checked the clock every time she tenses up . . . like that," Thelma added just as Lydia grabbed her middle and clenched her teeth. "It's about every four and a half minutes now."

Melody took Lydia's face into her hands and spoke firmly. "I'm taking you to the hospital, Lydia. You've got to calm down. I know you're hurt. I know you're upset. But right now you've got to concentrate. We can talk about the rest later. Are you hearing me?"

Lydia nodded, reducing her cries to an occasional sharp whimper. Matthew's heart ached to see the girl. She was little more than a child herself; a child with a broken heart and a baby coming.

Melody helped Lydia to her feet, at the same time asking Matthew, "Will you take us to the hospital?"

"Need you even ask?" He held up his keys and motioned toward the door. Lydia stopped and doubled over in pain, at the same time breaking into uncontrollable sobbing—again.

"Here," Matthew handed Melody the keys and scooped Lydia into his arms. "Open the door."

Melody opened the door. Thelma grabbed her coat, saying, "I'm going with you!"

"Be careful," Ben called.

Melody unlocked the car door, muttering over her shoulder, "My brother actually seems like a human being when he's sober."

"Yeah," Matthew said, carefully setting Lydia in the front seat, "I noticed that, too."

Thelma and Melody got into the backseat and Matthew drove toward the hospital, realizing he was nervous. Melody leaned forward, keeping an arm around her sister, talking softly to her. She noticed the peaceful quality of the scenery they passed, showing signs of Christmas celebrations still going on. Christmas lights twinkled in every window and on most rooftops, reflecting off the snow that covered everything except the walks and roads that had been cleared. Melody recalled what a wonderful holiday she had enjoyed. She imagined her and Matthew sitting in his family room watching a Christmas movie right now. For a few minutes she felt downright angry; but by the time they arrived at the hospital, Melody found that her thoughts had shifted. This *was* the spirit of Christmas. It was being there for her family when they needed her—not to enable their bad habits and coddle them through their bad choices, but to show unconditional love when *real* needs arose. Thinking back on her prompting to call her mother, she knew the Spirit had let her know she was needed. She didn't know what the night would bring. But she was with Matthew, and she was making a difference for the people she cared about. With that thought in mind and a prayer in her heart, Melody squeezed her sister's hand and convinced herself to stay calm.

Matthew pulled up in front of the hospital entrance and jumped out to get a wheelchair. He lifted Lydia into the chair, kissed Melody quickly, and said, "I'll park the car and meet you in labor and delivery—wherever that is. I'll find it. Hurry now."

"Thank you," she said and wheeled her sister into the hospital with Thelma at her heels.

Once Lydia was put into a hospital gown and attached to a few monitors, everything that had seemed urgent suddenly slowed down. Melody left Thelma with Lydia and went into the hall to wait for Matthew. Everything felt better once his arms were around her. "Is she all right?" he asked.

"Oh, she's fine. The nurses said she's definitely in labor and progressing, but it will be a while before anything significant happens." She looked up at him. "You really don't have to wait with me. It could take all night, and—"

"Hey, I want to be here. I've got tomorrow off. I'll be okay. I'm worried about you."

"Oh, I'm used to dealing with crisis." She looked suddenly concerned. "Did you call your parents?"

"I just did. They said to tell you they love you, and they'll be praying."

Melody tried to comprehend what that meant. "Matthew," she said, "I just have to . . . say thank you."

He chuckled. "For what?"

"For . . . everything. You've taught me so much. You've restored my faith. You've given me hope. You've made me realize my own worth, I believe. And you've taught me what Christmas is all about."

"I think Christmas just encompasses all those other things," he said, "in a roundabout way. And I don't think I did anything so remarkable. I gave you a few hints. But everything you learned came from within yourself. It was all there to begin with." He touched her nose with his. "I know, because I saw it there the first time I looked in your eyes."

"What? When you were picking my junk up off the courthouse floor?"

"Precisely."

Melody laughed softly. "I love you, Matthew Trevor." She kissed him quickly. "Merry Christmas."

"Merry Christmas," he repeated and kissed her again.

Chapter Fourteen

Melody went in and out of Lydia's room while the labor progressed. She kept Matthew posted, and around four in the morning she finally insisted that he lie down on one of the waiting room couches. The next time she went out he was asleep, and she let him be. After the local anesthetic took hold and Lydia relaxed, Thelma slept some in a recliner in Lydia's room. But Melody felt too restless, so she hovered close to her sister, offering support and encouragement.

During a quiet moment while Lydia stared into space with glazed eyes, Melody asked, "Do you want to talk?"

"I don't know what to say," Lydia admitted.

"We used to talk all the time."

"Yeah, well . . . things have changed a little since I was twelve."

"We're still sisters, Lydia. I know we have very different opinions and lifestyles, and I know it's been hard for us to understand each other. But I love you, Lydia. What happened back at the house must have been horrible for you. Talk to me."

Silent tears leaked into Lydia's hairline. "I thought he loved me. I . . . I thought if he just saw the baby . . . and held it . . . that it would change everything; that he would want to take care of us . . . and we could be a family."

Melody couldn't keep from crying herself as the reality of Lydia's disillusionments came to light. It was tempting to remind her of the choices she'd made. But Melody simply asked, "So, now what?"

"I don't know. I can't even think straight."

"You know, Lydia," Melody said cautiously, "having children didn't change our father. It only gave him somebody else to treat badly."

Lydia looked startled by the analogy, but she said nothing.

"What about the baby, Lydia? Don't get angry or defensive. Just tell me how you feel."

Lydia sniffled loudly. Melody handed her a tissue and wondered how she could blow her nose with that silver stud piercing the side of it.

"I know you think I should give it away," Lydia said, "and . . . maybe I should. But I don't know if I can."

"Nobody can force you to give it away, Lydia. But I believe the most important thing is what's best for that baby. If you truly love this child, Lydia, you will want to see that it's cared for in the best possible way." Melody lowered her voice and squeezed her sister's hand. "Do you want it to grow up the way *we* grew up, Lydia? Do you want it to always be afraid, to never have anything good? Is that what you want? Are you really ready to take care of a baby and give it what it needs?"

Lydia turned to look into her sister's eyes. Melody could almost feel her thoughts racing wildly, and she allowed Lydia the time to think it through.

Lydia finally said, "Mom told me you're going to marry this guy."

"That's the plan," Melody said carefully. "I hope everything turns out."

"How do you *get* a guy like that? I mean . . . he actually has a real job, right? And he's going to college?"

"That's right," Melody said, warmed at the very thought of Matthew Trevor. "Personally I think he's one in a million, and I'm not sure how I got so lucky. But the fact is, if you want to get a man who's decent and responsible, Lydia, you've got to be the same. And having an illegitimate baby isn't going to be a real plus in catching a good husband."

Lydia glanced away. After a minute she said, "Maybe I'm not ready to be a mother yet." She turned to Melody. "But you are."

It took Melody a moment to absorb the implication. She was so shocked that she had to remind herself not to open her mouth until she thought through her response very carefully. "No, Lydia," she finally said, "I'm not. I'm just learning how to take care of myself; it hasn't been easy. And now I'm going to take some time for Matthew and me to learn more about each other before we become parents. When the time is right, we'll have our own family. But you know, Lydia, there are people out there who have been married for many years; good people who can't have children of their own. God wouldn't make good people unable to have babies if he didn't provide a means for them to have a family. That is how his mercy works, Lydia. That's one way he compensates for the mistakes we make, and that's how it all balances out. Think of the joy you would give somebody. And think of the fresh start it would give you. You could start over and do anything with your future that you want."

Lydia turned away, apparently thoughtful. After several minutes she said, "I don't know if I could do it."

"Well, it has to be your choice. But ask yourself if what you're doing is for your sake, or if it's best for the baby. Just think about what I said."

As the sun was coming up, Lydia's labor intensified. With the nurse's instructions, Melody coached Lydia through her breathing and let Thelma sleep until they were preparing for delivery. Then they each held one of Lydia's hands as she gave birth to a tiny baby girl. Melody was so stunned by the experience that she could comprehend Lydia's desire to keep the baby. But as Lydia held the infant close, tears streaming down her face, Melody's heart ached for that baby. She knew Lydia would choose to keep the baby, and that meant an inevitably difficult future for both mother and child. It was downright heartbreaking to see the creation of one more dysfunctional generation.

It only took a minute for Melody to realize that something wasn't right with the baby. Lydia became panicked as a nurse gently eased the infant away and rushed her out of the room. Thelma stayed with Lydia while Melody followed the baby, noticing on her way past the waiting room that Matthew was still sleeping. She wondered why she didn't feel tired herself, but figured it would hit once the adrenalin stopped pumping.

As Melody watched her new little niece being cared for through the glass of the Intensive Care Nursery, her mind tallied the events of the last few days. Her world had taken drastic turns since Matthew Trevor had walked into it, and she was grateful. But this child only represented another layer of the heartache she was trying to free herself of. If it had been difficult to remain independent of her family's problems before, how could she ever teach herself not to care about this baby? She had seen her older sister's children suffer neglect until she'd called anonymously to make Social Services aware of the problem. Could she go through that again? Or, perhaps worse, could she pull Matthew into it? Would she ever be able to put away such concerns and just follow her heart?

When Melody finally got a chance to talk to the doctor, another layer of heartache settled in. As he walked away to tell Lydia, Melody was grateful that she didn't have to do it. She felt too numb to even pray. She wasn't even certain what to ask for if she did.

Melody pressed her face to the glass, watching Lydia's baby, wondering what would happen. She told herself she should go see if Matthew was awake. She needed him. But she couldn't motivate herself to even move. She was exhausted and starving, but she knew that eating or sleeping would be impossible at the moment.

"You okay?" Matthew asked and startled her.

Melody pressed herself into his arms, holding him tighter than she ever had. "I'm better now," she said.

"Your mother told me it's a girl." He looked through the glass at the baby, being examined by a nurse. "She didn't tell me anything else."

With her eyes focused on the infant, Melody muttered tonelessly, "That baby's addicted to hard drugs—just like her mother. I knew Lydia was smoking and drinking, and that has affected the baby as well. But she'd told me she wasn't doing drugs, and I was naive enough to believe her. If the baby survives, she could have any number of problems."

Unable to watch the baby suffering any longer, Melody turned her face to Matthew's chest and cried. He held her and whispered soft words of assurance, then he took her back to the waiting room and insisted that she lie down. He sat close beside her with his hand in hers, and with little effort she fell asleep.

Melody woke up abruptly, aware that time had passed. She lifted her head and saw Matthew sitting close by, reading from a Book of Mormon. She sat up quickly, then regretted it when her head swam.

"Hello," Matthew said.

"Is . . . ," she began, but didn't know how to ask.

"The baby's condition hasn't changed. Lydia's doing pretty well. I asked her if I could give the baby a blessing, and she actually said yes. My father's on his way up to help me."

"Is Mother . . ."

"She's with Lydia in the nursery right now. She's holding up pretty well."

Melody sighed, thinking how wonderful it felt to be taken care of; how nice it was to have somebody else handle the problems with a level head and a caring heart.

"How are you?" he asked.

"I don't know. I'm still too asleep to tell."

Matthew's parents arrived a few minutes later, and Melody marveled at their genuine compassion for someone they didn't even know. They found Lydia in a wheelchair in the nursery, tears streaming down her face. Melody wondered if observing an innocent child suffering from the consequences of her choices would have any lasting effect on Lydia.

Melody marveled at the way Matthew sat down close to Lydia, took her hand into his, and explained to her his beliefs in the power of the priesthood, and how his desire was to put the situation in God's hands. He also explained to her the need to give the child a name, and asked if he could do that as well.

Lydia nodded firmly. "Her name is Josie Marie."

While Melody listened to Matthew give this child a name and a priesthood blessing, she marveled over an aspect of sharing his life that she'd never considered before. She'd never even comprehended what it might be like to have a priesthood holder be a part of her everyday life. The words of the blessing were full of comfort and peace, though it seemed directed more toward those who loved this child than the child itself. When it was done, Melody noticed that Matthew seemed especially somber. While his parents were comforting Thelma, Melody asked him quietly, "Is something wrong?"

Matthew pulled her aside where he wouldn't be over-heard. "I've given many priesthood blessings, Mel, and I've had some pretty remarkable experiences, but . . ." He shook his head in disbelief.

"But?"

Matthew looked into her eyes, saying with conviction, "I could clearly see that baby's purpose, Melody. But I knew I wasn't supposed to say it. It's as if . . . Lydia would not understand at this point in her life. But . . . maybe I'm supposed to tell her . . . someday."

"I don't understand."

"The baby won't live much longer, Melody. She's already filled her mission." Moisture glistened in his eyes. "I could almost feel the presence of angels waiting to take her home."

Melody looked at Matthew, then at the baby. And she felt peace. In this case, she knew that death was by far the best solution. She only hoped that Lydia and her mother would eventually be able to accept that.

Later that evening, Lydia was standing with her face pressed to the glass when the baby died. Melody held her sister while she sobbed with more intensity than she had the previous evening before they'd come to the hospital.

Matthew took Thelma home, while Melody spent the night in the recliner in Lydia's hospital room. Little was said between them, but Melody felt it was important to be with her sister. The next morning, Lydia was taken directly to a drug rehabilitation center in Salt Lake City. Melody went home and slept for fourteen hours straight. She didn't even bother to wonder how she would make up the hours at work. A five-minute explanation to the manager had given her the time off she needed; and for now, that was all she cared about.

When she finally got the rest she needed, Melody called Matthew at work just to hear his voice. Then she called her mother.

"How are you?" Melody asked.

"I'm glad you called," she said. "I wonder if we could talk."

"Is it about money?" Melody asked.

"No, dear, it's not about money."

"Okay. How about if I come and get you and we'll go get a bite to eat. Then we can have some privacy." Melody didn't add that being under her mother's roof was simply disconcerting for reasons she didn't want to get into.

"That would be fine," Thelma agreed.

As Melody drove her mother to an inexpensive restaurant, it occurred to her that she had never considered the possibility of having an adult relationship with her mother. But the experience of taking her out of the house for Christmas dinner had shown Melody that there were always options. She could get to know her mother better without being exposed to the difficulties caused by her alcoholic brothers.

"So, what's up?" Melody asked once they had ordered their food. She had steeled herself to stay strong on her boundaries. She would not give financial support, and she would not expose herself to getting caught up in any of the dysfunction. Nevertheless, she was determined to listen to what her mother had to say, and she would try to offer appropriate feedback and possible solutions.

"Well . . . you see, Melody . . . I've been thinking a great deal the last few days." She chuckled uncomfortably. "I've probably done more serious thinking since Christmas than I have in the last thirty years all together."

Melody felt something close to butterflies erupt inside her. This was not what she'd expected. She leaned eagerly toward her mother, anxious to hear what she had to say.

"I wonder if maybe," Thelma's voice became tainted with sadness, "once I married your father I just stopped thinking. Maybe I even stopped feeling. And once he was gone, my life was so out of control, I figured there would be no way to change it. My children are grown, and I know it's not possible for me to change the way I've raised them. I mean . . . I never really thought about how my kids would turn out. I just took it one day at a time; all I could do was try to cope and keep them fed. But now . . ."

"But what, Mother?" Melody pressed when she hesitated far too long.

"I don't know, Melody. I can't explain what's going on inside of me." Thelma became emotional, dabbing at her eyes with her napkin. "Maybe it was seeing what a real family could be like. Or maybe it was having Christmas again for the first time since I was sixteen. Or maybe . . ."

Her emotion increased. "Maybe being with Lydia when she . . ."

Thelma cried discreetly while Melody held her hand across the table. "It's okay, Mom. I know it's hard."

For more than an hour, Thelma talked of wishing her life was different. She admitted to her concern that she might be contributing to the problems of her children—especially her sons, who were using her home as a refuge from responsibility. But she didn't know how it was possible for her to make any difference.

As Melody listened to her mother, she prayed inwardly for guidance in handling this appropriately. She felt certain that Thelma's sudden self-awareness was the result of many years of prayer on her behalf. It was a golden opportunity, but Thelma's struggles ran deep, with years of deeply ingrained habit beneath them. Nothing was going to change overnight. But Melody was being given the chance to plant some seeds, and if they were nurtured correctly, she felt confident that Thelma could find a better life for herself.

Melody gently offered to get Thelma some materials to read that might help, and she told her there were programs available to help people overcome codependency. Melody offered to make arrangements for her to get involved, and to help her get to the meetings, as long as Thelma committed to following it through.

"That would be fine," Thelma agreed. "But . . . what's codependency?"

Melody couldn't keep from laughing. Then she leaned over the table to hug her mother before she briefly explained the importance of not enabling other people's problems and allowing them to take advantage.

After Melody dropped her mother off, she went to the sporting goods store and found Matthew behind the counter, his head bent over some paperwork. The store was void of any customers, a stark contrast to the Christmas rush the week before.

"Is this where I can find some adventure?" she asked. He looked up with a grin and walked around the counter to greet her with a kiss and a hug.

"How are you?" he asked.

"I'm doing pretty good, actually."

"I take it you got the day off."

"I got the rest of the week off," she corrected. "The manager was great about it. And I can make up the pay with extra hours." She squeezed his hand. "Have you taken a break yet?"

"No. In fact, they owe me two."

"Good," she smiled. "I'd like to tell you about a miracle I just encountered."

In the car, Melody told Matthew about having lunch with her mother, and the things they'd said. He didn't seem all that surprised, as if he'd somehow expected her to have that much influence on her mother. While they were sharing hot chocolate and a pastry, Matthew asked, "And how is Lydia? Have you heard?"

"I called to check on her this morning. They told me she'd gotten past the worst, but it would take time."

Matthew nodded.

"I got permission to go visit her tomorrow. I was hoping we could work it into our other plans."

"I don't see why not."

"Matthew," Melody took his hand, "when Lydia was in labor, she implied that she wanted us to take the baby."

Matthew's eyes widened. "And what did you tell her?"

"I told her I wasn't ready to be a mother; not yet, anyway. I told her we would have our own family when the time was right, but . . ."

"But?"

"Well . . . I never could have done it, Matthew. I know it would have only enabled her problems. For her, it would have been an easy way out. She could still have seen the child and had contact, but I would have been taking care of it. And I wouldn't set myself—or you—up for that. But . . ."

"But?" he asked again.

"I guess just having to think that through somehow made . . ." Her emotions threatened. "I guess I'm just trying to say that watching that baby die was hard for me, too. I know in my heart it was the best thing, but . . ." She looked down and wiped her eyes, attempting to avoid smearing her makeup.

"Hey," Matthew touched her chin and looked into her eyes, "Josie Marie Morgan is one relative you're going to be with in the next life, Melody. When the time is right, *you* can do her temple work."

Melody felt so consumed with peace at the thought, she couldn't speak.

"And I must admit," Matthew added, "before I realized the baby wasn't going to make it, I had the same thought cross my mind."

"What thought?"

"About you and me taking care of her. Of course, I wouldn't have done it without a lot of prayer, and knowing it was the right thing. And it likely wouldn't have been. But . . . it did cross my mind."

206

Melody smiled at Matthew and squeezed his hand. She could never explain what that meant to her. Nor could she put into words that the greatest gift he had given her this Christmas season was the evidence of his love and acceptance for her family. "I love you," she said, hoping he understood how full he had made her heart.

"I was wondering," he said, leaning closer, "if you've thought about when you want to get married."

Melody hated the way an all-too-familiar uneasiness tightened inside of her. She could tell that he'd picked up on her hesitance before she'd had a chance to mask it. She had no choice but to say, "I . . . don't know if I'm ready for that yet."

Matthew reminded himself that he'd told her he would be patient. But instinctively he believed that her reasons for hesitating were related more to her inner fears than anything valid.

"Melody," he took her hand and held it in both of his, "I love you. I don't know what else I can say to help you understand that we have the ability to make it together—in spite of anything that might come along. But there is one thing I want you to think about."

"I'm listening," she said, wondering if she wanted to hear whatever he had to say.

"I get the impression that you're missing something, Melody."

"Oh, and what is that?"

"Faith, my lovely. Maybe you should just apply a little faith."

Melody actually felt angry. "You sound as if I don't even know what faith is. Well, I'll tell you something. I didn't get where I am without a whole lot of faith."

"Exactly," Matthew countered. "So if faith got you where you are, why is it so difficult for you to believe that it will get you where you're going?"

Melody opened her mouth to retort, but nothing came out. She closed her mouth and furrowed her brow. Matthew lifted his finger and gave her a sidelong glance as if to say, "I got you on that one."

After a minute's silence, he added gently, "I'm not saying that your concerns aren't valid, Melody. Going into marriage blindly and believing it will be bliss is certainly not the appropriate way to handle it. But we are two mature adults with some knowledge behind us—and more important, we have the gospel."

Still, Melody said nothing.

"Remember Jack and Hilary?" he asked.

"Of course."

"You know, after his accident, he didn't want to marry Hilary. He loved her. He wanted to be with her. But he was afraid of the hardship he might bring into her life. He was afraid that her love for him was partly pity, or that perhaps she was just being noble to not abandon him when he couldn't walk. But you know what? They're making it. They're happy. He's told me more than once that when it got right down to it, all he had to do was apply some faith and let go of his pride."

Matthew could see that Melody was absorbing something from his story, but there was still skepticism in her eyes.

"You know, Mel," he added, "Jack and Hilary are a success story, and so are my parents. I'm sure you can look around and find just as many—if not more—failures; relationships that fell apart for any number of reasons. All I ask is that you apply a little faith—in me, and especially in yourself.

"That's all I have to say," he concluded. "When you're ready to set a date, let me know. I was thinking Valentine's Day."

Melody made a noise of disbelief. It seemed just around the corner. "How about Halloween?" she countered.

Matthew smirked. "Easter?"

"The Fourth of July."

"Memorial Day," he said and laughed.

"How about next Christmas?" she asked.

But she wasn't prepared for the way Matthew pushed his face toward hers, whispering firmly, "Just how much willpower do you think I have?"

It took a minute for Melody to grasp his implication. Then she blushed. Before she could comment, he lifted his brows comically and added, "How about New Year's Day?" He glanced at his watch. "Do you think we could throw a wedding together in two or three days?"

"Not likely," she said. "In the meantime, why don't you just cool off and start counting the days until Thanksgiving?"

Matthew sighed and told himself to drop it, even though it was difficult for him to avoid thinking about his desire to marry her and begin their life together. But he'd told her he would be patient. He just hoped she would be willing to set a date sometime before Christmas. The thought seemed unbearable.

On the morning of December thirtieth, Matthew picked up Melody, then they went to get her mother and headed for Salt Lake City. They would visit Lydia, then meet his family for dinner, a visit to Temple Square, and the Nutcracker ballet.

"I don't think I have ever seen two lovelier ladies," Matthew said as he helped them out of the car, each wearing her new dress. Thelma blushed visibly and pushed her hand through the air with a little chuckle. Melody just smiled and took Matthew's arm.

Seeing Lydia was not what Melody had expected. The strain of detoxification showed on her face, but her eyes looked clearer than they had in a long time. Her hair was straight and smooth, her face freshly scrubbed. She wore no jewelry at all—even the stud in her nose was gone.

Matthew kept his distance, allowing the women a chance to talk freely. He was surprised when Melody summoned him, saying, "Lydia wants to talk to you."

Matthew felt nervous for reasons he didn't understand as he approached Melody's sister. "Hi," she said with a tentative smile.

"How are you doing?" he asked.

"Better, I think," she said. "I just wanted you to know that . . ." She got emotional. "Well . . . I don't I think I was really all the way there at the hospital. I didn't think too much about it when it was happening, but the last couple of days, I keep remembering the prayer you said for my baby. It's given me a lot of comfort. I just wanted you to know that."

Matthew sighed. "I'm glad it helped."

"And . . . ," Lydia began, then she seemed hesitant.

"If there's something you want to ask me, Lydia, feel free."

She took a deep breath. "I was wondering if you could pray for me, too."

"It would be an honor to give you a blessing, Lydia."

Without another priesthood holder present, Matthew couldn't perform a blessing for the healing of the sick. But he was able to bless her with comfort and hope, and to let her know that God loved her and was more than willing to help her as long as she made the right choices.

Lydia hugged them all before they left, and asked if they would come back soon. Then they met Matthew's family in the heart of the city, where they all went out together for a nice dinner. While Melody's heart was full from the evidence of Lydia's progress, she felt it overflowing to observe her mother taking in the experience like a child at a circus for the first time. Over dinner they discussed their plans for New Year's Eve. Matthew leaned over and whispered, "Or maybe we could get married."

"I think it takes a little longer than that to arrange a temple marriage, Matthew."

"Okay, Valentine's Day."

Melody scowled at him and kept her attention on the conversation going on around them. After dinner they all went together to Temple Square to see the Christmas lights. Melody wandered slowly among the trees with Matthew's hand in hers, thoroughly consumed with the beauty of her surroundings.

When they finally arrived at the theater, Melody was doubting that her heart could bear yet another positive experience. She felt certain that with time, life would level off and achieve a balance between the struggles of the past and the absolute elation she had experienced through the holidays. But for the time being, she was content to relish every moment.

She was full of butterflies as the ballet got underway, and knew from Thelma's expression that her mother felt much the same way. Melody absorbed the sights and sounds, wanting to hold them inside forever. With her hand in Matthew's, she felt like Cinderella at the ball. Everything was perfect—for the moment. But would midnight come? Would reality set in and release her from the beauty and wonder she had discovered in her life?

Melody felt her emotions hovering close to the surface as the plot of *The Nutcracker* began to unfold. The Cinderella analogy struck deeply as it seemed to coincide with the story of a young girl experiencing a dream where a doll had become a prince, and everything was perfect and magical. Melody didn't know the end of the story yet, but she knew that eventually—like all dreams—it would end. And the reality of life would take over.

During intermission, Melody almost felt depressed. The ballet was half over. And then what? Of course, they had plans for New Year's Eve. But they would both go back to work. Matthew would start classes. Life would go on. She would be struggling to help Thelma overcome her codependency. And with any luck, she could actually make a difference for Lydia at this point in her life. But the holidays would be over, and the drudgery of everyday living would take over.

As the second half began, Melody turned her mind to prayer. She begged her Father in Heaven to help her get beyond this discouragement and doubt, and to find peace. Of course, she'd been praying for that very thing for days now; but if she had any faith, as she had so haughtily claimed to Matthew, she had to believe the answer would come.

While her senses were consumed with the theater, the dancers, the costumes, and the music, Melody's mind wandered. She began to tally the events in her life since the moment Matthew Trevor had stopped to help her in the courthouse. And now she was here, holding Matthew's hand, his ring on her finger.

It was somewhere in the middle of the *Waltz of the Flowers* that Melody began to feel the warmth growing inside her. There was no tangible thought that changed her outlook; she simply knew something she hadn't known a moment ago. And with that knowledge came an undeniable peace.

She turned to look at Matthew and found him watching her more than the ballet. But looking into his eyes, she saw something she'd missed before. The answers she'd been looking for were there all along. Just as Matthew had suggested, they were within herself. The trick was in looking at herself through Matthew's eyes. And yes, she did have faith enough to believe they could make it together. She didn't have to dread the coming of midnight, or fear that the dream might end. For Melody, the good things in her life were not temporary. Whatever life dished out, she knew that as long as she remained true to her covenants and trusted in her Father in Heaven, she and Matthew would be together forever. Sure, life would go on, and it would bring struggles. But they had conquered struggles before—not only on their own, but together. Matthew had proven his ability and willingness to handle the situation with her family, and he had certainly proven his love and commitment to her. And most important, her Father in Heaven had let her know that marrying him was the best thing for her. She felt certain there was no man on earth as right for her as Matthew Trevor, and by heaven and earth, she would not let him go. She would do everything in her power to be a good wife to him, and a good mother to their children. And as long as he held her hand, there would always be something to look forward to.

The ballet ended just as Melody had predicted. The dream came to an end. But the tears she cried were of perfect joy; not only for being able to partake of this unforgettable experience, but to know that her future was bright.

"What's wrong?" Matthew asked after the orchestra had played their final note and the applause had finally died down.

"Nothing," she insisted, wiping at her tears. "It was so beautiful. I didn't want it to end."

Matthew hugged her. "Well, you know what, Melody Noel? Christmas will come again. And some things just never lose their magic when you keep a place for them in your heart."

Melody nodded, and they walked outside holding hands. The magical feeling hovering inside Melody multiplied tenfold as they stepped out into a sea of snowflakes, floating to the earth as if pieces of heaven were overflowing.

Melody lifted her face skyward and laughed. "I love snow!" she declared. Then she looked into Matthew's eyes. "And I love you, Matthew Trevor."

"I love you, too," he said, hugging her tightly.

Melody smiled. "How about April fifteenth?"

"What about it? That's when taxes are due."

Melody wrinkled her nose. "Okay, April fourteenth. It's right between semesters, isn't it?"

It took Matthew a moment to figure out what she was talking about. Then he found it difficult to speak.

"Well?" she said before he got a sound out. "Do you want to marry me or not?"

Matthew just smiled and kissed her. *Like the kiss of an angel,* she thought.

Epilogue

Matthew had come to the courthouse to talk to his father. But as he put his coat on and hurried out of the building, memories of meeting Melody became so close he could almost taste them. Walking down the courthouse steps in the cold only intensified the images in his mind, making him all the more anxious to get home. It had been more than a year since their first encounter in the courthouse. In a way it seemed like only yesterday, but at the same time, he felt as if they'd been together forever.

Matthew made a quick stop first, and came in the door with a bouquet of flowers behind his back. The apartment smelled of pine and spices and a warm oven. The lights on the tree illuminated the tiny front room with a magical glow. But he couldn't find his wife.

Knocking at the closed bedroom door, he heard her shriek, "Don't come in!"

"What are you doing in there?" He laughed to hear indications of her scrambling around to hide something.

"Don't ask questions this close to Christmas," she called back. "Okay, you can come in."

Matthew opened the door and laughed again to see her sitting in the middle of the bed, surrounded by gifts and wrappings. Wearing a green and red plaid sweater, she looked like some kind of Christmas elf. Matthew cleared a path on the bed with a sweep of one arm. Then he knelt on the bed to kiss her long and hard before he pulled the flowers from behind his back.

She gasped. Then she grinned. "But you said you already got me a birthday gift, and—"

"Oh, these aren't for your birthday," he said, kissing her again. "That comes later. These are for our anniversary."

"Anniversary of what?" she asked, inhaling the bouquet's fragrance with her eyes closed.

"It was a year ago today that I asked you to marry me."

"So it was," Melody said, smiling at him.

"How did finals go?" he asked, taking off his tie.

"Pretty good, I think," she said. "I'm glad they're over."

"At this rate, you might actually get your teaching certificate before I pass the bar."

"It takes a little more time to become a lawyer than it does a teacher, but . . . I'm thinking I might need a break in there somewhere."

"What for?" he asked.

"Oh, my gosh," Melody gasped, looking at the clock. "We're supposed to be at Mom's in half an hour."

She rushed to the closet in search of something to wear while Matthew took the flowers to the kitchen to put them in water. "Hey," he called, "put on that red dress!" When Melody emerged, wearing the dress she'd bought last year for Christmas, Matthew declared that she got more beautiful every day.

Together they went to Thelma's house where she had a birthday cake, gifts, and balloons.

In the past year, Thelma Morgan's home had gone through as drastic a transformation as her life. Matthew

216

had often declared that it was Melody's influence on her mother that had made a difference. And maybe it had helped. But Melody knew that no matter what opportunities were offered a person, it took something good from within to take hold of them and help them make the most of it. Melody was living proof of that.

After attending some classes and group therapy, and reading several books, Thelma had made a plan to take control of her life. She'd gotten a part-time job at a care center cafeteria, and quickly discovered that she loved it. She spent an equal amount of volunteer time there, visiting with the elderly and helping them with little things. This new independence, together with getting out of the house, had done wonders for Thelma. She got herself a car and started going to church.

When summer came, Thelma had given her sons a list of things she wanted done around the house, with fair warning that if they didn't get up and earn their keep, they would be on their own. When time passed and they didn't comply, Thelma maneuvered getting them out of the house. Then she had the locks changed and set their belongings on the front lawn. The last Thelma had heard from Ben and Joe, they had gone to Mexico to move in with their sister. Melody felt certain they would all do beautifully being dysfunctional together.

Once the boys were gone, Thelma became a cleaning maniac. She went from one end of the house to the other, throwing things out and scrubbing from top to bottom. Melody and Matthew helped with some painting, both inside and out. Lydia moved back home, although Thelma made it clear that she would not tolerate any laziness, bad language, drinking, or smoking in her home. Lydia didn't have a problem with that. She was completely drug and alcohol free—she wouldn't even drink anything with caffeine in it. And she hadn't been home long when she caught the cleaning bug herself. Once the house was put in fairly good order, she took it upon herself to keep it that way while Thelma spent her days at the care center. In the fall, Lydia started classes to get her high school degree, then she had plans to attend Utah Valley State College. She wasn't going to church, but she was holding down a job. And she actually had goals for the future.

Even though Melody had become accustomed to the changes in her mother and sister, she regularly thanked the Lord for all that was good in their lives. It was difficult to take something for granted that she had gone without for so long. Even now, the reality that she was having a birthday party at her mother's house, feeling no inkling of embarrassment or discomfort, seemed something close to a miracle. And Melody was grateful.

Matthew's parents arrived a few minutes after they did, seeming almost as comfortable in Thelma's home as they did in their own. Once the gifts had been opened, they all piled into the Suburban to go out to dinner. Since Colin was driving, Matthew sat in the backseat, his arm around Melody.

"I have a birthday present for you," she whispered.

"It's not *my* birthday," he chuckled.

"I know, but . . ."

Matthew tightened his arm around her. "There is absolutely nothing I need, Melody Trevor. I am the happiest man alive."

Melody looked at him with exaggerated disappointment. "Well . . . I can't take it back. If you have everything you need, then . . ."

"Then what?" he asked when she couldn't hold a straight face.

"Then I suppose you're telling me you don't need a baby?"

Matthew was too stunned to speak. Then he laughed. He held Melody tight and just laughed.

"What's going on back there?" Colin hollered.

"Should we tell them?" Matthew whispered.

Melody shook her head. "We'll tell them Christmas Day."

"It's a secret," Matthew hollered back, then he kissed Melody and she whispered, "Merry Christmas."

Author's Note

Traditionally, in our home, we have our big Christmas dinner on Christmas Eve, and for dessert we always have Pumpkin Cake Roll. And since my skills are more in writing than cooking, it always tastes better than it looks. Here's the recipe; I hope you enjoy it. And have a great Christmas!

PUMPKIN CAKE ROLL
3 eggs (beaten for 2 minutes)
Add: 1 cup sugar
      2/3 cup pumpkin
      1 tsp. lemon juice
Add: 3/4 cup flour
      1/2 tsp. nutmeg
      1 tsp. baking powder
      1 tsp. cinnamon
      1 tsp. ginger

FROSTING
6 oz. cream cheese
4 Tbs. butter
1/2 tsp. vanilla
1 cup powdered sugar

(Leftover frosting goes great on sugar cookies.)

Pour into a greased and floured 9 x 13" pan. Bake at 375 degrees for 12 minutes. Cool 15 minutes, then roll in dish towel dusted with powdered sugar. Make frosting and spread in middle, then re-roll (without the towel).

Photo by Nathan Barney

About the Author

Anita Stansfield published her first LDS romance novel, *First Love and Forever*, in the fall of 1994, and the book was winner of the 1994-95 Best Fiction Award from the Independent LDS Booksellers. Since then, her bestselling novels have captivated and moved thousands of readers with their deeply romantic stories and focus on important contemporary issues. *A Christmas Melody* is her tenth novel to be published by Covenant.

Anita has been writing since she was in high school, and her work has appeared in *Cosmopolitan* and other publications. She views romantic fiction as an important vehicle to explore critical women's issues, especially as they relate to the LDS culture and perspective. Her novels reflect a uniquely spiritual dimension centered in gospel principles.

An active member of the League of Utah Writers, Anita lives with her husband, Vince, and their four children and two cats in Alpine, Utah. She currently serves as the Achievement Days leader in her ward.